P9-CRC-199

Dr. Bird's Advice for Sad Poets

Evan Roskos

Houghton Mifflin
Houghton Mifflin Harcourt
Boston New York 2013

Houghton Mifflin is an imprint of Houghton Mifflin Harcourt Publishing Company.

www.hmhbooks.com

The text of this book is set in Photina MT Std.

Library of Congress Cataloging-in-Publication Data

Roskos, Evan.
Dr. Bird's advice for sad poets / Evan Roskos.
pages cm
Summary: A sixteen-year-old boy wrestling with depression and anxiety tries to cope by writing poems, reciting Walt Whitman, hugging trees, and figuring out why his sister has been kicked out of the house.
ISBN 978-0-547-92853-1
[1. Depression, Mental—Fiction. 2. Family problems—Fiction. 3. Poetry—Fiction.] I. Title. II. Title: Doctor Bird's advice for sad poets.
PZ7.R71953Dr 2013
[Fic]—dc23
2012033315

Manufactured in the United States of America
DOC 10 9 8 7 6 5 4 3 2

4500405748

To Rin
and
Laura

And henceforth I will go celebrate any thing I see or am,

And sing and laugh and deny nothing.

—Walt Whitman

1.

I YAWP MOST MORNINGS to irritate my father, the Brute.

"Yawp! Yawp!" It moves him out of the bathroom faster.

He responds with the gruff "All right." He dislikes things that seem like fun.

I do not yawp like Walt Whitman for fun. Ever since the Brute literally threw my older sister, Jorie, out of the house, I yawp at him because he hates it. My father says reciting Walt Whitman is impractical, irrational. My father says even reading Walt Whitman is a waste of time, despite the fact that we share his last name. My father says Walt Whitman never made a dime, which is not true. I looked it up. Not on Wikipedia but in a book that also said Walt used to write reviews for *Leaves of Grass*—his own book!—under fake names.

Who does that? Walt does!

The perfect poet for me. I'm a depressed, anxious kid.

I hate myself but I love Walt Whitman, the kook. I need to be more positive, so I wake myself up every morning with a song of my self.

Walt says:

> *I celebrate myself, and sing myself,*
> *And what I assume you shall assume,*
> *For every atom belonging to me as good*
> *belongs to you.*

I say:

I am James Whitman.

I define myself and answer the question that was asked with my momentous birth!

I am light! I am truth! I am might! I am youth!

I assume myself and become what you assume!

I leap from my bed, bedraggled but lively! Vigorous, not slowpoked and sapped with misery (despite my eyes and aching teeth, which grind all night)!

I bathe, washing the atoms that belong to me but are not me.

I brush my teeth. Away! Away! Gummy grime of six hours' sleep! Six hours of troubled dreams will not slow my hands as they scrunch my cowlicked hair into an acceptable—no, *vital*—posture!

I adorn a bright shirt—sunburst of red on white, a meaningless pattern. But so is a sunset! So are clouds! I choose low-cut socks and cargo shorts with enough pockets to carry all my secrets.

It is April, the first warm day of the year, a day where I can loaf and lounge and contemplate a spear of grass lying in my palm. A day when the sun has to work hard to burn off the mildew of a dillydallying winter that beat me to a pulp. A day when I forget depression, forget my beaten and banished sister, Jorie, living alone somewhere. A day to YAWP! out across the moist air of the park on my way to school. I do not mind the grass tickling my ankles. I do not mind the chill because I have my old green hoodie infused with the musk of the prior fall, the dander in the hood, the history of sweat!

Ah, my self!

I sing through the park, greeting trees, stopping beneath them to stare at the way the morning sky filters through the newborn leaves.

I chitter at squirrels, who celebrate themselves.

"Hello, my nutty friends!"

Contemplating my demeanor, they hold their tiny paws to

their mouths. But I need to keep walking, to keep moving, to get to school before my mood falls apart.

Walt says:

> *Dazzling and tremendous how quick the sun-rise*
> *would kill me,*
> *If I could not now and always send sun-rise out of*
> *me.*

Some days I feel like I'm on the verge of supernova-ing.

Other days I'm a leaf of grass.

Every day I miss my sister, expelled from home and school with just a few months left. No prom, no graduation, no celebration, no gifts. A metaphorical footprint on her ass after years of literal bruises on her body put there by my mother, the Banshee, and my father, the Brute. I loafed in my room while she raged on the front lawn, cursing the very house for the miserable nails that held it together to protect me and my mother and yawp-hating father.

I hug trees, dozens on especially bad mornings when the walk to Charles Cheeseman High School feels long and insufferable.

When I hug trees, the bark marks my cheek and reminds me I'm alive. Or that my nervous system is still intact. The trees breathe all the time and no one really notices. They take in the air we choke on. They live and die in silence. So I hug them. Someone should.

When people see me hugging an old maple tree in the park, they probably think I'm a kook. I am okay with that, though I'd prefer they not let me know what they think of me. Let me be, I ask.

Like Walt says: *I cannot say to any person what I hear . . . . I cannot say it to myself . . . . it is very wonderful.*

I also hug trees to apologize to them. When I was in fourth grade, Jorie and I threw chunks of scrap bricks at a dogwood tree. Brick can really do some damage. Tears the thick skin right off and exposes pale tree flesh. When we stopped for a moment to collect the larger brick bits, my sister looked real close at what we did and said she felt horrible.

"The tree is crying!" she said.

"A tree's a tree," I said, ready to adjust my technique for some real damage. "It can't feel anything."

But Jorie said that just because the tree couldn't feel or speak or think didn't mean we should throw bricks at it. She left me in the backyard. I spent an hour trying to put bark back on the vulnerable tree.

2.

ANOTHER TERRIBLE HIGH SCHOOL DAY awaits, though I'm calm after embracing four trees that will outlive me. As I step out of the park onto the pale sidewalk, I see Beth King across the street. The sight of her reminds me what a girl in a spring-friendly outfit looks like: *wonderful.* (Imagine butterflies so drawn in by a bright flower that they forget how to fly; that's the feeling I get from Beth in her warm-weather outfit.)

I pause to hug one last tree before jaywalking. I want Beth to notice me but not the crazy part of me. So, I keep my hand on the tree trunk and let her move ahead so I can follow her.

As we walk, I see a bird in the street. It's not flying away, and I know birds tend to hop a lot when scrounging for food. This one flaps one little wing like it's injured. I look at the bird and at Beth and back at the bird. For a moment I think it would be awesome if she noticed the bird and showed some kind of concern, but she's texting on her phone very intently.

A car passes and I cringe—but it misses the bird, who flaps its wing frantically. I need to save the bird! No one else notices these things!

If I can grab the sparrow (or finch or swallow) and get it to the other side of the street, then Beth will see I'm a sensitive, bird-loving man! Huzzah! A heroic grab of the bird and a well-timed "Yawp!" will win her heart!

I jog at the perfect angle so that I can grab the bird, dodge oncoming traffic, and arrive light-footed on the opposite curb. Maybe even a somersault! This will be the greatest how-we-met story ever!

I dart into the street and make a quick grab for the critter. I need to hurry to get through the lane and over to the other sidewalk, so Beth can cheer me and hug me and appreciate the acrobatic Olympic double-roll hop I've just somehow initiated.

I'm airborne!

I'm really a superhero!

I think I've been hit by a bus!

The horizon flips around—twice, I think. The bird crumples in my hand. Suddenly I cannot see clearly. I hold on to the bird but lots of things hurt.

The diesel smell of the bus is the smell of my shame. The kids on the bus are laughing at me. I know none of them thinks this is a serious issue. The bus driver comes out and screeches at me.

"What the heck are you doing?! Running out in front of me? How'd you miss a big yellow bus?"

I hold up the bird.

"I was saving a bird."

The bird's not struggling to flee my grip. The bird might be dead!

"That's a damn Tastykake wrapper, you idiot!"

So it is.

I look over and Beth is gone. She didn't see me almost die. Or she did and didn't think it was that important.

3.

EVERYONE AT SCHOOL is calling me Short Bus.

A kid in the hall says, "High-five, Short Bus!"

I hold up my cast and the kid tries to bump our forearms in mock camaraderie.

At least I'm famous, right? (How many people in history have thought "At least I'm famous!" for doing something stupid? Probably tons, thanks to YouTube.)

Before homeroom, my friend Derek tries to make me feel better with the only wit he can muster.

"Heard you tried to jump on the short bus to be with your own kind."

I should mention he's my only real friend.

Derek and I have known each other since preschool. He's a year ahead of me, though he still lowers himself to be seen with a high school junior now known as Short Bus. Derek tends to get along with tons of people, which I admire but also find curious. I'm not sure how he gets people to like him. People just do.

Sometimes I think that people automatically like Derek because his dad died. That seems mean, but there it is. It's not just that with Derek, though; he listens and laughs and never says bad stuff about anyone behind their back. Derek's dad died when Derek was in fifth grade. It was my first funeral. Derek's relatives swarmed his mother and sisters, but kept telling him he was the man of the house in a way that seemed very official and menacing. Derek told me a few days after the funeral that he didn't know what being a man of a house meant. We speculated that he now had to sleep in his parents' bed and go to his dad's job.

Derek has a permanent marker ready to sign my blank cast. (My mom offered to sign it, but that's the kind of hit to my already terrible reputation I wouldn't survive.) I don't watch what he's writing because his proximity to me is unnerving. When people get this close to me—doctors, teachers, waiters—it puts me on edge. Derek doesn't seem to care how close his body is to anyone in the world. In fact, it's like he's allergic to clothes. He plays basketball shirtless. He mows the lawn shirtless. He even grills shirtless. He sits around his house in nothing but boxers, even when his mom and sisters are around. He's usually one awkward movement away from flashing his ball sack.

I am allergic to exposing my skin, which I think is the more mature approach to life.

I look down at my cast, about to say something about his sneeze-inducing cologne, and see that he's written something he finds hilarious.

Something that made me cry in third grade.

We had a sub because our teacher was in an accident or got hepatitis or something. So we were not learning anything but were instructed to choose one of three activities: read quietly, sleep quietly, or play hangman (quietly). Derek came up with a puzzle and three of us were guessing. After a few guesses, here's what I saw:

_A_ES IS _ _IEND_ESS

When I realized what it said, I gave up and went to a corner, where I allegedly cried, and as a result gained a short-lived reputation as a crybaby. (I was saved from this reputation a few days later when Benny Gordon cried so hard in dodgeball that he wet himself. The human body is a horrible thing.)

So now the phrase JAMES IS FRIENDLESS shouts huge letters across my forearm, leaving no room for sympathetic girls to draw hearts. This week just sucks.

"If I'm friendless, why are you hanging out with me?" I ask, trying to wipe the marker off before it dries.

"I tell people you're my sociological experiment. Also, that your mom pays me to be nice to you."

Later, in Physics, I am distracted by Beth because she seems to be distracted by me. Or by the reputation-crushing message Derek left on my cast. Whatever the case, the girl who didn't look my way when the grill of a bus ruined my week is now shamelessly watching me calculate force with a dull-tipped pencil. Maybe she wants to confirm that I belong on the short bus.

Of course, I *want* her to look at me, but now that she is, I feel very objectified. This is probably how Beth would feel if she knew that I stared at the way her just-long-enough black hair stayed so nicely tucked behind her nearly perfect ears.

When class ends I am torn between an impulse to walk out of the classroom at the same time as Beth and my impulse to avoid human communication until my cast gets removed. On the verge of what promises to be a major anxiety attack, I decide to dart out the door. Secretly, though, I'm happy when I hear a girl calling out my name as I walk down the hall. Who wouldn't be?

I don't respond right away, which is why she calls out "Short Bus" for good measure. The hallway ignites with laughter.

I've played it a bit too coy, perhaps.

"Yes?" I turn around and try to calm my stomach butterflies.

"You're the guy who got hit by the bus, right?"

I laugh and hold up my arm and tell her my names is James, that only enemies and strangers call me Short Bus.

"You're Jorie's brother?" she asks.

"Yes." I was not aware that she knew my sister. "Why?"

"She—can we walk? I have gym and am notoriously late."

(Is it wrong that when Beth mentions gym I imagine her changing in the girls' locker room? Or is it wrong that I stop myself from imagining this?)

We walk.

"Your sister used to submit tons of poems to the *Amalgam*."

"What's that?"

Beth laughs as if this question is common.

"The school literary magazine, which no one reads. Jorie gave us stories sometimes too, but mostly poems."

"I did not know this." I think back. Jorie never told me about her publications. Maybe she assumed I read them and didn't like them. I want to call her and say that I didn't even know the magazine existed.

"She sent us so much stuff and she was, honestly, better than most of the people who submit. Even better than the other editor, who writes all this lame suburban angst. His parents are loaded and still married—what kind of angst could he have?"

"Yeah." It's the only thing to say to a green-eyed girl who might love poetry as much as I do.

"He didn't write at all, and then he started reading Sylvia Plath and junk and tried to take over the magazine. Amazing how exposing sophomores to certain poets causes radiation sickness to their own writing."

I get the sense that she really, really wants to talk about poetry. I should say something about Whitman. Oh, what? What? I'm blanking. Crap!

"Lots of the poems we published were written by your sister," she mercifully continues. "We just made up different names to make it seem like the school was being represented well."

She can tell I'm shocked, and then I'm more shocked because her fingers touch my forearm for one billion nanoseconds as she giggles. She's looking at me. I am not invisible. I couldn't invisible-ate myself if I tried.

"No one ever caught on?" I ask.

"Nope."

"The school is big," I suggest.

"Plus, no one really reads." Beth's laugh includes a charming snort. "Well, only a small percentage of the school. No one went out of their way to find out if Jake Growling really was a student here. Or Jane Air. Or Willy Hamlet."

"*Willy Hamlet?*" I laugh louder than I've ever laughed at school.

"I guess I wanted to get caught." She bites her lip. She's a cliché of beauty!

We walk, and walking is good when it's not just me weaving through the happy and dumb.

"I knew she wasn't going to be around forever," Beth continues. "She was due to graduate and all."

She awkwardly squints down the hall as if she sees a recognizable face. I think she's just trying to avoid the topic of my sister's expulsion.

"You want me to write some poems or something?" I ask.

"Oh! No. I was wondering if you could see if she finished

this big piece she was working on. It was a graphic story. Pictures and words graphic, not violent graphic."

"Yes. I can."

No, I probably can't. I never snooped through Jorie's room when she still occupied it. Going in there now is like grave robbing.

Maybe I can write Beth a thousand poems fueled by the image of her face right at this moment! Her face wears a delight and a shyness and a beauty that I imagine is unnatural for a girl named Beth who plays field hockey and shows up late to gym.

"Can you get it to me quick?" she asks, checking her phone but returning her gaze to me rapidly.

I want to be honest and say no, but who am I kidding? This is the only recent conversation I have wanted to last more than twelve seconds.

"Yawp."

"Huh?" she says.

"I mean yes."

"Great!" Beth hops with glee. (Later, in my slow-motion memory, I will see hundreds of strands of her hair floating down lit by sunlight even though we're indoors. I will see freckles that I never noticed before. I will see how her lips could easily be described as plumlike.)

But right now she says she's late for gym, and spins and runs off. I want to think something romantic because I'm convinced that something will happen with me and her. But damn my brain and my eyes—all I can think of is how wonderful her butt looks in those pants.

4.

SINCE SHE LEFT, I have been in Jorie's room only twice, to reclaim CDs from the cluttered maw of her desk. Those visits—during the day, when the room still seemed inhabited—lasted seconds.

Once I'm sure my parents are asleep, I go into Jorie's room and turn on the small lamp by the door. The shade has crude skulls cut into it. The skulls' shadows shiver a bit on the walls. The lampshade is one of her late-night projects, for sure. Jorie enjoyed enhancing perfectly functional items. She drilled a hole in the side of her jewelry box that allowed her to shake out two earrings. She wore them regardless of whether they matched or not.

My mother has cleaned a little and my father righted the fallen bookcase, but the room still has that Jorie energy. She could be asleep beneath the rumpled bedspread right now. Clothes, papers, and books are strewn everywhere. She hated leaving used dishes in her room, but she'd walk on notebooks and pens and art supplies. Jorie never worried about keeping certain valuables protected. She returned a number of my CDs with catlike scratches or coffee rings and didn't understand why I was annoyed.

But all this flotsam and jetsam is secondary to my purpose: tonight I'm looking for words and not-violent graphic images. I look through the half-dozen journals on her bookshelf. They stand too neatly for the room. It's likely my mother has already skimmed through them, looking for evidence of sex and drugs and hatred. Instead, she saw lots of drawings. Pretty surreal fantasy stuff—fat fairies in skimpy clothes, spiky flowers covered in bees smoking cigarettes, dragons with butterfly wings and buck teeth. Some are from years ago, according to the dates (which are just as ornate as the drawings). One of the journals has text, which I only skim in order to feel a bit less guilty. It seems to be a story about a girl and her dog planning to help people in need but never getting around to it (at least not for the first few pages).

There are some sketches of the girl, her dog, and a bloated-looking frog-man who might be a villain or the principal of our school. Or both. The girl is Jorie-like. I can tell by the hair. Jorie liked to keep her hair relatively short and use rubber bands to make little ponytail spikes randomly on her head. I look over at her dresser and there's still a huge container of tiny multicolored rubber bands. She went through thousands. Sure enough, the girl in this journal has spiky hair and bony knees (another very Jorie detail).

I'm struck by my first real memory about Jorie—one that has the arc of a story, anyway, and is not just a flash of images or feelings. When I was four, I was having a recurring nightmare—something about the Super Mario Brothers chasing me and making me eat huge bowls of cereal. After waking from that dream, I cried a lot, but I covered my mouth to keep from alerting anyone. I was afraid that the Mario Brothers would exact revenge if they knew I'd told on them. (The revenge, of course, would be to jump on my head before feeding me to Yoshi.)

One night Jorie came into my room and said she heard me crying. I told her about the dream and she told me about a dream she had where she was a teacher.

"Who wants to be a teacher?" she said. "I don't want to be in school all day teaching people stuff I already know."

I can't remember what I said. Probably nothing. Jorie didn't always make sense to me when we were little.

That night, to help me sleep, Jorie gave me one of her stuffed animals—a shark with these huge felt teeth.

"This shark eats bad dreams," she said.

I carried it everywhere for months because it was soft and because it really did make my dreams go away.

Tonight, thinking of that shark, I put the journals back—loosely and disorganized, the way my sister would prefer.

I have a moment of profound, stomach-aching, palm-sweating guilt. I have many moments of guilt, actually, but this one feels acute and fresh. I'm not supposed to be in this room at night when my sister isn't around and isn't coming back.

I'm among the reasons she's not here.

I know she wasn't happy or safe here, but maybe if I'd helped her . . . . There are certain things that I did and certain things I failed to do.

Then, life decides to freak me the heck out: My cell phone vibrates with a text from Jorie! There's no actual text, just a close-up image of some orange berries on thin limbs against an intense blue sky. I reply, asking if she's okay, if she needs anything. She's probably far away, falling asleep. I wait a few minutes but get no response.

I decide to leave the room forever, but then I step on The Board. A perfectly inconvenient floorboard located in a place where it cannot be avoided. It acts as an alarm, letting out the kind of jagged belch that can rouse even the heaviest of sleepers (i.e., my father).

As Jorie probably did many times, I freeze. I am convinced that I can remove my weight from the board without creating a follow-up—and more alarming—belch.

I have a few memories about this damn floorboard and the fights it started, but for the moment I begin to slowly lift my foot. Microscopically slow. In my head, I know I'm making no sound. I pretend it's outer space in my sister's room. Things happen but sound waves don't travel.

In reality, though, the sound is not unlike a starving lion about to chainsaw through a thousand crying baby caribou.

"What the hell is going on?" My father's voice cares not for walls. He speaks, you hear it.

I dart for the door, but once I'm in the hallway, the Brute spots me.

"What are you doing in her room?"

I turn around and see my father standing there—he's an unimposing man this late at night. He sleeps in tightie-whities and an undershirt with yellow pit stains. It's not that he's a messy man—out of shape, unattractive, bearlike—or anything. He's normally a shaven, successful man who lunches with people. He deals in commercial real estate. He once grabbed Jorie's forearm so hard it bruised.

But in the cool glow of the evening, this is my lame father. His knees look girlish and bony. He reeks of cigarettes. He is angry.

I say I haven't done anything in Jorie's room.

"I'm gonna bolt that room shut. Now go to bed. You're rude, making noise at *whatever-the-fuck-o'clock* it is."

I apologize and go to my room, ready for another sleepless night. I don't even mutter a "yawp" before closing the door.

5.

FOR A YEAR, I've been seeing an imaginary therapist. Her name is Dr. Bird. She is a large pigeon, human-size. She wears no clothes. Because she's a bird. I imagine that we're meeting in a dim therapy office. She doesn't have a desk or a chair. She will pace and circle and bob her head while I talk.

Pigeons strike me as good listeners—they discern the voices of mates over the cacophony of the natural world. They move the right way too. A pigeon's head-tilts suggest the kinds of things that I imagine therapists say: "Really?" or "How did that feel?" or "Tell me more." Plus: one intense, glassy black eye staring at me, the neck-bob of agreement, the puffing of feathers when I'm being evasive.

Today, I start by telling her about the photo I got on my phone.

"It was a tree with orange berries and a blue sky. From Jorie."

Dr. Bird bobs her head while she does a circular walk.

"It makes me feel like she misses me."

Dr. Bird pecks something on her notepad. I imagine the notepad filled with important scratches and claw marks.

Dr. Bird asks if I sent a picture back to my sister.

"I didn't. Should I have?"

Do birds have shoulders? Dr. Bird seems to be shrugging hers.

She asks me what I would photograph.

This, of course, is a trap. She's going to use her highly intelligent pigeon brain to interpret my answer. (Don't laugh—pigeons are smart.)

"I don't know. I have these weird moments when I see things—ordinary things—and I just find myself staring at them. Or just part of them. I stared at the lower left part of a stop sign one day. It had a dirty handprint smacked into it, but no one would see it unless they stood just where I was standing with the sun just where it was floating. It was about time and light and perspective. And dirt. I want to take pictures of stuff like that."

Dr. Bird says that this is interesting. She's wants me to be interesting, to have interests, and to be interested in staying alive. I do not tell Dr. Bird I want to kill myself sometimes, but she knows. She's up in my head. She perches on the power lines of my thoughts.

"Why not trees?" she asks. "That way you're capturing the happiness of the trees that you feel and doing something other than hugging them."

"It's not *happiness.* It's *calmness,*" I correct. Making a distinction between happiness and calmness is the closest I can come to admitting that I never feel what I assume is happiness.

"That's right, I'm sorry." She jams her beak into the crook of her left wing, going after a bug or the perfect wording for her advice. "But I think if you took pictures of trees and put them in your room, then you would fall asleep and wake up with trees. That might help you combat some of the late-night anxieties you feel."

Dr. Bird is a damn genius. I tell her so and she coos.

6.

DEREK PICKS ME UP at my house and says I have to accompany him to the drugstore out on route 38.

I agree but immediately question why we have to drive to a drugstore so far away.

"So I get to drive more." Derek loves to drive his '99 Honda Accord with the custom dents and brand-new sound system.

He spends at least seven minutes looking for a song on the radio.

"Radio?" I say. "How quaint!"

"I left my CDs at home."

"What are CDs?"

"Dick." He laughs.

Inside the store, I ask about our purpose.

"I need to buy some condom-ents."

He is not funny.

"You are not funny," I say.

"I need you to be my prophylactic wingman. Distract the pharmacy girl so I don't have to do the snatch-and-grab."

The snatch-and-grab: whereby a man, or Derek, walks past the condoms and grabs a box without looking so as not to attract unwanted attention from drugstore employees, many of whom are old women or young women with bad teeth. The downside of the snatch-and-grab is accidentally ending up with condoms that do not fit one's lifestyle.

"What do you need condoms for?"

"I've been seeing this woman."

"Woman? How adult-sounding."

"She's twenty-one."

"Shut the hell up!" I yell in the store, causing the elderly man dusting off the register candy to smirk at me.

"Serious. We've been doing it for about a month. I want to spice things up by using protection. Maybe even try the ribbed or swirly kind."

"You haven't been using protection?"

"Hell no! You know that method where you pull out?"

"I am not familiar with that method."

"Of course not, because you haven't even kissed a girl where she pees."

"Pulling out is a method for knocking a girl up and, on a more minor note, making a bit of a mess. It's not helpful for avoiding pregnancy," I say. "Also, what if she has the Herp?"

"She doesn't have the Herp! She's engaged."

"Your logic confounds me."

"If she had some kind of disease, she wouldn't be engaged."

"Yeah," I say, "that makes no sense."

"You'll get to meet her at Mike Redman's party."

"Do I know Mike Redman?"

"You don't?"

I know Mike Redman by name, reputation, and haircut. He tends to lead a pack of athletes around school. They all have faux-hawks and started growing beards in unison recently. He's not an asshole, as far as I know. He could be. I've never had any interaction with him whatsoever. He's never randomly locked me in a gym locker and neither has he wedgied me, knocked my books around, or, in a more contemporary bullying stereotype, stabbed me with a toothbrush shiv carved during Home Economics then posted a video of the assault on Facebook.

"I'm not sure if I've been invited," I say.

"Invited? Who invites people to parties?"

"People with manners." I hold up a bottle of Perky shampoo and ask, "Do you think if you rub this on your man boobs it will make them perky?"

"You are coming to the party with me. It's gonna be crazy! I was at one he had a few weeks ago—half the school went."

"He had a party a few weeks ago, and he's already having another? What's he celebrating?"

"He's celebrating being alive and popular." Derek holds up a box of hair coloring. "You need to bring out the burgundy in your hair. Chicks love burgundy hair." He holds the box close to his mouth and wiggles an obscene tongue at the fabulous and happy woman on the cover.

"I will go to the party with you as long as you promise never to do that in my presence again."

"Agreed!"

We walk around trying to look nonchalant. It's ridiculous. Derek makes a lap around the store to see if there are any employees near the condoms.

Like every other drugstore I've been inside, this one employs about seven part-time elderly people and two or three teenage girls. It's basically the most embarrassing place to buy condoms.

"Okay, there's a young Asian girl working the pharmacy

counter, and the condoms are just off to the left. So I want you to talk to her so I can grab what I need."

"You will owe me so big."

Where Derek gets his ethnicity information baffles me: the so-called Asian girl is actually a Latina.

I go up to the consultation window and immediately blank on what to say. Derek needs at least twenty-five seconds to crouch down, get his condoms, and move on. So far I have killed four seconds.

"Picking up?" The girl—woman—asks.

"Um. Yes." What the *hell* am I doing?

"Last name?"

"Walker." This is not my last name.

"Walker?" She turns and begins looking at the various plastic bags hanging on the wall behind her. A whole wall of remedies, none of them mine.

She's analyzing the names closely. Perhaps I've lucked out and there's no one named Walker getting medicine here.

I look over to the left and see Derek *pondering*. Is he comparing brands?!

The woman comes back with a bag.

"Devin Walker?"

"Um."

"For Viagra?"

I am outraged that she doesn't whisper my name and my medicine! I should complain to the manager, but then I realize that I just have to tell her it's not my medicine.

"No. That's not me," I say.

"Oh—that's the only Walker I have over there."

"Yeah, that's definitely not me." I laugh nervously like a guy in a beer commercial trying to hide shenanigans from his hot girlfriend.

The girl—woman!—puts the Viagra back. I shoot Derek a look and wave my arms frantically, but now he's considering what looks to be flavored lubricant.

You don't deserve flavored lubricant! I want to yell.

The woman comes back and says I should check with my doctor for my prescription.

"Good idea." I agree. "It's allergy medicine. I have bad allergies. Viagra doesn't help with allergies, does it?"

Derek is preparing for wild strawberry-flavored sex, and I suffer from fake postnasal drip.

7.

I ASK DR. BIRD if it's normal to dread social gatherings. She says to be cool, but it could just be a "coo." It's not hard to tell; I just may not want a clear answer.

I am not good in crowds of people. The very thought of going to Mike Redman's party makes me sick for three days. Not physically sick, exactly. The brutal tease of anxiety burns my stomach. Perhaps my stomach lining will dissolve completely. There's no specific element of a party that makes me afraid to leave my house. But from the moment that I agreed to go—an agreement that came during a gleeful, carefree moment without the serious thought a party invite should inspire—I began to think of a dozen other things to do instead:

Clean room

Put winter clothes away

Rearrange books

Learn how to cook a soufflé

Learn CPR

Go see a movie alone

Try to contact Jorie and hang out

Only the last entry is really worth pursuing, but in the days that follow my agreement to go to the-party-I-was-not-invited-to, I come up with more and more stupid things (dust, buy new shoes, learn how to skateboard) to avoid being in a house that is not mine, surrounded by people I do not know, talking about things I do not care about, drinking copious amounts of alcohol that will make me barf.

Like Walt says: *A dread beyond, of I know not what, darkens me.*

I tell Derek on Thursday that I'm not going to the party. I almost tell him I'm not feeling well, but realize feeling sick more than twenty-four hours in advance is not a reasonable excuse.

"Why not, man?" he asks.

"I just think my parents won't let me go."

"Tell them you're going somewhere with me."

"They'll probably tell me to be home by ten or something. And I know you'll want to stay out later than that."

"Tell them you're seeing a late movie. You can stay out past midnight."

See, this is how *desperate* a multiday anxiety assault can make me: I construct complex reasons not to go somewhere, involving my parents, who probably wouldn't even notice or care if I was out for an evening, and lie to my best friend, who wants to include me in something fun.

I'm on a streak of something like eighteen weekends of not going out.

"Whatever, dude. I'm not going to beg you."

Derek walks off to class and I go to Physics, where Beth might ask me about Jorie's writings, which I have not yet found.

But she doesn't bother me in class. In fact, I am very aware that she doesn't look at me at all, since I spend most of the class looking at her.

"Whitman!" Mr. Hobblestein yells. "Stop staring out the window! You're not going to learn about the laws of physics by looking out there—it's not a closed system."

Some of the physics nerds laugh. And why not?

I blush, afraid everyone will know that the window is not my focus, but no one cares about my weirdness. Not even Beth, who looks grumpy or tired or bored.

After class, I purposely take my time loading up my books

so I can walk out with Beth, but her lab partner lingers, so I decide to just *bolt.* I should go through the entire week without talking to her. I shouldn't draw attention to my failure to have something to give her.

In fact, it's probably my fault that she's in a dark mood.

God! Do you see the ridiculous things my brain does? What would Whitman do? Loaf and ponder. Jerk off in a field and write a poem about it.

I need to hug a tree. I need to yawp.

In the hall I shuffle along to my next class but can't help turning around a couple of times to see if Beth is trying to catch up to me. She's not. But she is just a few yards behind me, so I stop to get a drink at a fountain and try to sense her pace to know when to stop drinking. The water misses my mouth and drenches my cheek, so when I stand up to talk to her—ready with a convincingly surprised voice—I have to wipe my face like a first-grader struggling to drink from a milk carton.

"Hey, Beth."

She doesn't hear me as she passes, so I make a bold move. I smack her book bag the way friends might. Playfully. We're friends! We're having fun! Huzzah!

She spins and takes a billion nanoseconds to recognize me.

"Oh. James! Hi."

"Sorry. I'll leave you alone if you want. Just thought you looked blue."

"No. Tired. Tons of stuff going on. Just one of those weeks."

"Yeah. I never really have *one* of those weeks. Most of my weeks are like that."

"That sounds unfortunate."

"You get used to it. Grimness, blobbiness, fogginess."

We walk quietly.

"No luck on the search for Jorie's graphic story," I say.

"Bummer." She's about to dismiss me then and there.

"But I will keep looking. I have to make short forays in there."

"Why's that?"

"Parents don't like me going in. I guess they're pretending something."

Beth's about to respond but looks at her phone instead.

I agitate my brain's detritus in search of a funny story. Something to cheer Beth up. I've got nothing! I don't know enough about her to say anything witty and personal and funny.

So I go with the thing that's one step above commenting about the weather: *asking about her weekend plans.*

"Well, I was supposed to go to a party," she says, "but I might not get there."

"What party?"

"Mike Redman's?" she asks. "You know him?"

"Oh. Yeah, I heard about his party."

Yes, I'm the guy that fails to say, *I'll be there! Let's go together!*

"Are you going?" she asks.

"One of my friends asked me to go. But."

Beth waits for me to offer some explanation. I think of a few that won't make me sound like a loser.

I try: "My parents are a little strict with the curfew thing."

"Oh."

"Are you gonna be there, though?"

"I want to go, but I've got this drama with my boyfriend. It's a huge pain in my huge ass."

She laughs and I fight an urge to comment that her ass is not huge.

"Is it like an episode of *Drama Mavens?*" I ask.

"Exactly like that! Only stupider." Thank god she laughs.

"Well, then you need to go to this party. Isn't that how the people on the show would solve their problems? Get all the people together at a social function, drink a little, have it out in a big melodramatic shouting match?"

"Totally! Someone falls in the pool, someone gets rufied,

someone comes out of the closet, someone becomes emotionally vulnerable."

"You know, I don't think I've ever seen that show. But it sounds awesome."

Beth laughs and admits she's never watched the show either, which makes the snobby part of me very happy.

"If you're gonna be there, I'll try to get there too." This is the bravest thing I've said in weeks, but the butterfly monster in my stomach roars. Will I just end up telling Beth tomorrow that I'm not going? Will she be disappointed or echo Derek's "whatever, dude"?

"What role will you be playing in my little *Drama Mavens* plot line?" she asks.

"Oh. I guess I'll be the new friend who your boyfriend thinks is threatening but turns out to be harmless."

"Nah. You should be the guy with the accent who everyone thinks is mysterious but who just turns out to be poor."

"What kind of accent?"

"A mixture of Russian and Vietnamese."

"I'll work on that."

For the rest of the day my anxiety is unbearable because I have agreed to go to a party that I've already backed out of and the girl who convinced me to go has a boyfriend and drama and might not even be the kind of girl I like even though I think she's really, really cute and reads poetry.

But what would my week be without a massive cloud of worry? It would be a different week. And my weeks just aren't different.

8.

WHEN I CALL DEREK to say I've rechanged my mind, he doesn't act surprised. In fact, he doesn't pick on me or call me a dick or anything. Just says he will pick me up at eight.

By seven-forty-five I've narrowed my outfit choices down, but every time I put on a shirt I feel like a dork. The arm cast doesn't help. I want to look normal, inconspicuous, approachable, but also somewhat invisible. I have a black Radiohead shirt with a bunch of white houses on it. It suggests I have good taste in music but also that I need to let everyone know I have good taste in music.

My other option is a gel-toothpaste-green polo shirt that makes me feel minty fresh. A nice color but not conversational. I imagine Beth passing me by because she can't think of anything to say about my outfit.

For pants I have the choice of corduroy (which feel about a year past freshness) or jeans (always classic) or khakis (too formal).

I have only one pair of shoes, casual sneakers made of hemp that are in desperate need of new laces but will suffice for this evening.

Derek shows up and I throw on jeans and my Radiohead shirt as he comes up the stairs.

"Are you decent?" he calls down the hall.

I tell him to come in.

"Your parents give you any shit about tonight?" he asks.

"I'm planning an out-the-door announcement of 'Going to the movies with Derek.' We'll see how that works."

"They love me; it'll be easy."

Derek stares at my shirt for a lingering second.

"I know you're not a fan, but it's either this or that." I point to the minty shirt.

"I don't care what you wear. I just think that band is boring."

"Is the *shirt* boring?" I ask. "Because it's not like the shirt plays music."

We laugh. It's going to be a good night.

At the front door I yell my perfected line down to the family room. The Banshee and the Brute will have less than ten seconds to evaluate and respond. Still, they rarely give me crap about going anywhere because I rarely go anywhere.

Derek trots outside, confident that there will be no restrictions placed on his evening.

But rather than "Okay" or "Be safe" or "Who are you again?" I hear footsteps, and then both of my parents are looking at me like I've lied to them. Which I have, but they shouldn't know that.

"Where are you going?" my father asks.

"Movies. With Derek. He's outside." I point to the porch and Derek waves and grins like a goof.

"Be back by eleven," my father says.

"The movie might not be done by then."

"You should see a shorter movie then."

"Or you should see an earlier one," my mom says.

"Why do I need to be home? Are we getting up early tomorrow?"

"It's your curfew." The Brute points at a plastic clock on the wall.

"I've never had a curfew."

"You have one. It's eleven."

I consider staying home. My eyes burn like there's a weird,

tiring, hot dust in the air. Derek will kill me if I bail. He'll also kill me if we have to leave the party to get me home by eleven. Either way, he'll attempt to murder me.

I look down at my shirt. What a stupid shirt! I'm a stupid kid. Why do I think I deserve to go to a party anyway? I'm just going to clam up, sit in a corner, watch the clock, not drink, not smoke, not enjoy myself. I'm going to end up hating how happy everyone seems.

"Let me tell Derek," I say.

I go outside and tell him that I have what is known as a curfew.

"Whatever. We'll go and I'll bring you back. You need to get out of this house."

"Maybe I can say we're going to a theater that's far away?"

"Rule Number One of Teenage Happiness: *Less detail makes for an easier lie.* Just tell them you'll be home."

"*Will* I be home?"

Derek sighs, then goes inside my house. I watch him talk to my parents, charming them, being the kind of son they might like. The Banshee tends to respond well to him for some reason. She has very easy rules for people who are not her kids.

My father, on the other hand, is suspicious of everyone. But whatever Derek says seems to get us permission to leave. In the car I ask him what he said.

"I said you would be home disease-free and sober by midnight."

"You're a goddamn magician."

Mike Redman's house overwhelms all of my senses. The air smells of cheap beer and burnt hamburgers. Bass thumps the floor, rattling expensive vases. I immediately look for a wall to stick my back against. I get a soda from a cooler out on the deck but not because I'm thirsty: the can will protect me. I tend to need talismans in crowds. Tortilla chips, napkins, my cell phone, all work well.

Someone acts like I bumped into her, but actually she bumped into me. I say sorry automatically, because I always say I'm sorry automatically.

I look around for recognizable faces at this classy affair. It's strange how similar but different people look outside of school. The ladies seem to be wearing more makeup than normal and the gentlemen seem to be wearing their dressier baseball caps. My T-shirt feels a little too hipster, but at least I'm not wearing a baseball cap.

When people at school talk about parties they've been to,

I tend to glaze over as the list of who-said-whats carries on and on. Now my anxiety, boiling away at my insides, makes it hard for me to really take in details. I'm constantly looking at the time, wary that the hour of midnight will suddenly happen and I'll be hours away from home and destined for punishment.

Derek doesn't ditch me right away, which is a nice surprise. I fully expected this to be a night of flirtation for him, even though he does have a sexual mentor now. He's amazing to watch at a party. He manages to hold conversations while constantly checking his phone and acknowledging people who pass through the room.

Derek tells me to have a beer so I have a beer. It's not peer pressure: it's survival. I realize that the risk of a vicious panic attack is greater than the risk of getting caught beer-breathed on my return home.

The beer is cold and erases the soda film from my teeth.

The beer and anxiety make time skip around.

9:29—Someone yells out, "You are my number one *bitch friend forever!*"

9:35—Derek says: "I think if I lived next door to secret

Muslim terrorists who were going to attack America, I would figure it out."

And then: "But I think that if they knew me, if they got to know me, they'd probably reconsider what they're planning to do. I feel like I can get along with lots of different people."

8:37—Beth appears. As if by magic. She comes around the corner acting like she's been here forever. I stare her down, hoping that we'll make the kind of eye contact reserved for people who are meant to be together. Imagine my shock when she comes right up to me and says hi in the kind of peppy-drunk way that I've only wished to experience.

"Hi yourself!" I yell over the distorted music urging everyone in the house to bop their heads and make terrible dance moves in shadowed corners.

"How long have you been here?" she asks, somewhat hyper.

"I looked for you, briefly. I'm a little overwhelmed by this whole thing."

"It's loud in here. But not crazy. I expected craziness!"

"Well, now you're here. Maybe these people will get crazy!"

8:36—I'm in the kitchen, wishing I had stayed home. The

kitchen is bright white, the brightest room in the house, and I'm the guy standing next to a bowl of broken chips atop grease-soaked red napkins.

9:15—Beth and I drink and talk about things we never knew we had in common. We recite lines from movies. Beth tells me she wants to be a journalist. I tell her that journalists don't appreciate the nuance of language. Beth says poetry doesn't mean anything for anyone besides the poet and maybe five of the ten people who read it.

"Poetry is like self-abuse," she says.

"You mean like suicide or something?"

"Masturbation!" she yells over the din of the party.

I blush.

9:02—Beth notices me staring a little too long at her boobs. She adjusts her shirt by doing that pulling-back-of-the-shirt-shoulders thing, but it's all loose and slips down again. I get hot in the face. I want to tell her that she's got great boobs, but there's no polite way to say so. I want to talk about the lines that make the curves and the shirt that makes the other lines. Is this making sense? Basically, I want to compliment her tits! How can I not, when they're being offered there, plentiful, wonderful, well lit even in the dull house with dull people who don't read poetry!

YAWP!

9:47—Derek says he has to go pick up his lady friend but promises to be back.

8:50—Beth offers to get us more beer and I ask for a soda to pace myself. I make a great joke about cutting back on my drinking to make a good example for my parents.

9:21—Someone yells out: "I'm not sure these are my pants!"

Someone else: "Well, give her shoe back then!"

9:54—Beth and I have a conversation with a few other people that seems to have no beginning and no end. It involves why I don't eat chicken, something strange Beth remembers from a third grade spelling bee, this guy's secret crush on his second cousin, and another girl's crush on the aforementioned cousin-lover.

10:15—Beth introduces me to her fashionably late boyfriend, Martin, a delirious-looking, corduroy-wearing dude with a goatee. I laugh at his pants. Out loud. I just laugh at them, but I can't explain why they're so funny.

10:01—Beth calls her boyfriend and learns that he's been at the party for an hour but that he didn't come find her.

"*Drama Mavens?*" I ask.

"All the *fucking* way, my friend." She touches my broken arm for two billion nanoseconds.

We're friends! I note the time and the position of the moon and the song playing and I look at her eyes not her cleavage and her eyes glisten but she seems to have trouble with my eyes so she looks away. My eyes are probably cloudy, sad, mean, boring. Not blue enough or brown enough or bright enough.

10:33—I explain to Martin, with the help of four beers in a body that doesn't drink much, that I work with Beth on the literary magazine.

"Poetry is for chicks and gays." He laughs because he's trying to lighten the mood by saying stupid things. This makes sense because we're drunk and having a wonderful time.

"Don't be mean, Martin," Beth says.

"How'd you break your arm?" Martin asks.

"Saving a Tastykake from a bus."

Martin thinks I'm joking.

"It was a sentimental Tastykake."

10:45—Derek shows up with my sister, Jorie. I'm enraged! Is this his lady friend? Is this is his brilliant way of telling me? Should I have known this? I'm racing through all the things I should say, but my anger is showing. Jorie gives me a hug that calms me down even though I want to shake her and punch him.

What are they doing? They cannot be in love!

I'm not sure why not.

Then he introduces me to a lady who is *not* my sister. Her name is Sally Something. She is his lady and she is apparently Jorie's boss at Fillmore's, a chain restaurant famous for naming burgers after ex-presidents and side dishes after their vice presidents.

I am relieved more than I can describe. His lady is the kind of lady I expect Derek to have been seduced by. A lady a few years older than us, conspicuous at a high school party (maybe she's a college dropout). She's got blond hair and a tight shirt and legs and things, but who cares?

Jorie is here!

Jorie!

9.

THE REST OF THE PARTY is just me and Jorie and Beth and sometimes Derek when his lady runs off to use the bathroom to do some coke or to trigger an allergy attack (either way, she seems to have nasal issues). I'd like to celebrate SaraSally-Something and assume she's just living the life she wants to live, but something tells me doing coke at a high school party is not what she dreamt of when she was little. Then again, who knows. Everyone has different dreams.

But the real celebration, the wondrous, YAWP!-worthy, loafing-on-the-grass joy, stems from my sister's presence. I'm not even upset that she can only stay for an hour because she has to work in the morning.

"On my feet all day." She shows me the worn bottom of her shoe.

"How do you live?"

I want to hear that she's got money and a nice place to live, that her friends are helping her. I want to hear that she misses being at home. Instead, she complains a bunch about things like a small bathroom and a loud landlord. She has no car. She bought a bunch of thrift store clothes. She's learned to live on less.

"Do you want me to pack a bag for you?" I ask. "From the closet or your dresser?"

"Mom didn't throw out my clothes yet?"

"No. Why would she?"

"She throws out my clothes *all the time.* Says they're old or ripped." Jorie leans in and whispers comically loud, "Even though they *aren't* old or ripped!"

"They haven't touched the room, really." I hesitate to mention the things that have been touched.

"Why did you get kicked out?" Beth asks, too loudly it seems. There's a reasonable pause that I threaten to fill with an honest answer, but then Jorie cuts me off.

"Oh, typical stuff. Politics. Religion. Arguments about Ultimate Fighting Championships on Pay-Per-View."

"Bummer," Beth says.

I think that it's fortunate Beth and I are buzzed. Beer will prevent us from exploring certain conversational threads.

"You ever finish that graphic story thing?" Beth asks. "I've got nothing for the last issue!"

I can feel my tenuous connection to Beth dissolving—she won't need to talk to me if Jorie can just hand over this mysterious graphic poem.

"Left everything in my room, Beth! It's there with all my best socks and bras."

"I could write you some stuff," I offer. This makes as much sense as me offering to conduct brain surgery on myself, but I need to say something to prevent Beth from revealing that I went into Jorie's room.

"Yeah, you should let my brother give you stuff. He reads lots of Walt Whitman. He should be able to crank out something good enough to fill twenty pages."

I laugh because I feel like someone should laugh.

And then it's all over. Derek comes back and says his lady needs to leave, which means Jorie needs to leave. The invisible magic of our conversation fizzes away. I hum a sad song as Beth strolls off to find Martin.

I hug Jorie and ask her to send me more photos.

"I don't always have a computer and I'm gonna have to get rid of my phone soon. But I saw those berries and the sky was so blue! I thought it would cheer you up."

"It did," I say.

"Did you need cheering up?"

"I always need cheering up," I say as cheerfully as I can.

"It should be okay, though, at home? It should be calm and cool."

I smile in a way that suggests that things are not cool, that I want her to come home, but what can I say in a stranger's house to my sister who lives somewhere strange and has no money and no car and works all day so she's no longer getting knocked around and screeched at by our brutish banshee parents?

"It's okay," I lie. "Things are okay."

10.

ON RANDOM SATURDAYS, my mother conscripts me to clean the house. We never clean the entire house, just certain sections intensely. The worst cleaning, of course, is the bathroom. Or the kitchen. It's a tie, really, because both rooms involve lots of bleach or ammonia. Never both.

"Your grandmother nearly *died* once because she poured a bunch of bleach into the bathtub and she didn't know that I had poured a bunch of ammonia in there already."

My mother always uses cleaning gloves—bright green. She gets a pair of them every month. Her cleanliness is a divine neurosis.

Today we're cleaning the kitchen. I offer to shake crumbs out of the toaster. It's the least annoying job I can do with one working arm. Plus, I can stretch it out for twenty minutes without suspicion.

"When I was very little," my mom says while halfway inside the fridge, "it was easy to clean the fridge because we didn't have as much food. We grew our own veggies and had plenty of fresh fruit from local places in the summer, but we didn't have much food in the fridge itself. Your grandfather hunted and we got a freezer for the venison, but I think I was ten by the time that happened."

I try not to encourage many details about my mother's childhood since it gives her opportunities to tell me how grateful I should be.

After cleaning the fridge from top to bottom, she asks me to help her pull it away from the wall so we can vacuum the back. The air behind the fridge smells hot and tastes coppery. The dust makes me feel a little sick. It's all dead skin, cobwebs, crumbs, cigarette ash. Who knows what else.

While my mom drags the vacuum hose along the coil, I notice a piece of faded red construction paper poking out from under the fridge. When she's out of the way, I squat down and carefully pull the paper.

"Is that from you kids?" my mom asks over my shoulder.

The paper has two handprints of different sizes with our

names under each. Red construction paper, white paint handprints.

"I remember doing this," I say.

"Was that for Dad's birthday?"

That I cannot remember. Jorie and I wore old, paint-speckled dress shirts, put on backwards so that we each had to button the other's shirt. I remember trying to paint a lion with brown paint for the mane and yellow for the face. Jorie helped me make the lion's nose and eyes. She painted a huge tree on multiple pieces of paper that we taped together. About six pieces of blue. No! It was three blue for the sky, three green for the grass. She made the trunk with brown paint and for a moment I even remember getting mad because she used up the rest of the brown before I could try to make another lion. Then she let me help her with the tree; I was happy. I drew birds the way my second grade teacher taught me—two black curves. All the birds I drew looked like distant seagulls. Jorie painted the tree, gave it a bird's nest. She painted a cloud and a sun. We spent hours. I might be making up all sorts of details, but here with my mom I feel like everything happened exactly that way.

What the hell happened to that tree?

We painted a bunch of things that afternoon, but this handprint thing might be the only thing we kept.

I think it was for Valentine's Day. Or my parents' anniversary. Or maybe it was my dad's birthday. Should I be worried I can't remember why we did it?

"I should give this to Jorie," I say, forgetting for too many nanoseconds that Jorie lives somewhere else.

I really really really just thought I could go upstairs and give this to her.

11.

THE SCHOOL SECRETARY'S NAME is Mrs. Berry, but she smells like cigarettes. Extremely so. I wonder if she knows it.

"I need to speak with Mr. Kunkel," I ask on Monday morning when I should be off to third period.

"*Principal* Kunkel," she corrects without making eye contact, though I'm not sure what she's doing since her desk is relatively paper-free and her computer monitor is off. Maybe she's staring at her next cigarette.

"Sorry."

"He's not in." She looks at me.

I leave her alone to count down the nanoseconds to her next break.

I'm not sure what to do next. My plan is not very involved. All weekend, I was reminded of how Jorie was living in some kind of limbo. I sat in my room and worried about her. But not in the usual way I worry—not with pacing and sweating and nonsense thoughts. I had a *pure* worry for her. It felt rational but sick. I thought of terrible things happening to her: people breaking into her apartment, stealing her few valuables, menacing her physical well-being (though I stopped myself from overimagining this). Then I imagined her living under a bridge somewhere, becoming a local sob story: "Girl Under Bridge Wears Trash Bags, Eats Stray Cats; Parents Refuse to Help."

Maybe this was late-night, fatigued thinking, but I thought that if she could come live back at home, she might be safer. She might be able to save money, get a car, live more comfortably. She could write and draw and try to be a better version of Jorie—a more family-friendly version. I imagined fun dinners. I imagined her complimenting my parents. I imagined we'd all be better at being a family.

Plus, I could actually help her this time, instead of turtling up during the awful moments.

Dr. Bird—who doesn't charge extra for late-night therapy—said I should simply ask my parents to let Jorie come back home.

I disagreed.

Dr. Bird said I might just be scared to bring up the situation.

I disagreed again, but we both knew she was right.

"I'm going to work this the other way around," I said. "Get

her back in school, then back at home. Maybe the school can force my parents to let her move back home, even. Like, on the condition that she's living at home she can finish out the year."

Dr. Bird stretched her neck and glared at me with one solid black eye. She said she was surprised by my naiveté, a word I never thought a pigeon would know.

"I need to do it this way, Dr. Bird."

She dug her beak into the crook of her wing.

"If you need to do it this way," she said, "it means you need to learn how to talk to your parents in a different way."

Dr. Bird bobbed her head, then fluffed out her feathers.

Session over.

So, I'm at the principal's office, desperate to plead my sister's case.

I go back up to Mrs. Berry.

"It's kind of urgent that I talk to someone today."

"If you're having *personal* issues, your guidance counselor can help."

"It's not that kind of urgent."

The secretary snaps some gum. Or maybe it's her teeth clacking in disgust at my refusal to take advantage of school services. I expect her to tell me that the counselors get paid good money to deal with my problems.

"The vice principal is in." She gestures to an office.

Vice Principal VanOstenbridge looks like a less successful version of my father. His shirts seem perma-wrinkled; his glasses constantly slide down his nose. He speaks with the voice of a shy kid ordering his own food for the first time. He's pale, too, paler than normal people who are pale for a particular reason (nausea, fear, the flu). He's paler than the *Twilight* vampires, but less pale than an albino. Also: sweaty. He's a sweaty, translucent creature. Like a jellyfish without the poison stingers. He's like the lame jellyfish that never makes it on nature shows—no tentacle stingers. Just a clear disk that gyrates regularly to keep moving. Who would watch a show about that?

"I guess I can talk to him." Who knows if he even has the power to do what I want.

"Sit and wait there." She gestures at a brown wooden chair next to his office door.

While I wait for VP VanO, I begin to worry that I'm unprepared for this meeting. I came in ready to make demands but not ready to discuss specifics. VanO is the kind of person who thinks school is *great fun.* He loves school functions, PTA meetings, Back-to-School Night, pep rallies and bonfires. But VanO seems like he might crack if demands are made in his presence.

I might have to use finesse. But I don't have finesse. I have panic attacks and my family's genetic tendency to talk too fast when upset.

The student who comes out of VanOstenbridge's office seems pale. Is VP VanO contagious? I have no time to fear it, as I'm being welcomed in by his noodley arm and an all-lip smile.

Walt Whitman would find a way to celebrate VanOstenbridge. Walt found something to celebrate about everyone.

"You have a very clean office," I say while sitting down.

"Thanks." He sits behind his desk. "What can I do for you?"

"I'm here to ask about my sister. Jorie. You might remember her?"

"The first girl expelled from this school in its history. Yes. I remember."

If I could read people's faces I might know if VanO would be sympathetic to my plea.

"Well. I wonder if there's any chance she can be allowed to walk in graduation."

VanOstenbridge tilts back in his chair. The resulting squeak kills any sense of contemplative authority the gesture would normally carry. I expect his chair to whisper a request for oil.

"This chair," he chuckles. "Older than me!"

I blurt out my mastered fake laugh. It sounds exactly like this:

Heh!

"What you're asking, what you're *really* asking, is that the school admit it did something wrong by expelling Jorie. And I'm not sure the school board or Principal Kunkel and I would be able to do that."

"Don't think about it as admitting a mistake. Fighting is wrong—we all know that. No one wants to pretend that she didn't get into a fight. It's just—she deserves to have a chance to graduate with everyone else."

"And why does she *deserve* that? Do you know what she did, exactly?"

VP VanO gets a file from behind his desk. It seems odd that he'd have a file on my sister at the ready, but if she really is the first girl to get booted out, maybe everyone in the administration reads the file each morning to remember the worst student ever.

"She got into a fight with Gina Best," I say. "Essentially."

"Well, *essentially* it wasn't a *fight* so much as a *beating.*" VanO twitches his mouth, mouse-like. "It was an *ambush.*"

I shake my head. "She hit the girl's head against the locker. But it wasn't an ambush."

"You know that your sister sent Gina to the hospital?"

"Yeah, but everyone knows that was a joke. It wasn't serious."

"You know that Gina's head was smashed into a locker." He looks at me. "You know that Gina went to the hospital as a result."

I try to look at him, but my eyes find everything else in his office quite interesting.

"That's *not serious?*" he asks.

"She didn't get stitches or staples or anything."

"Would you like someone to smash your head against a locker? To see if it feels serious?"

This feels like a threat, and suddenly my assumptions about VP VanO seem very, very wrong. He's pushing back. I'm not even pushing.

"Most people think it was a pretty tame fight," I say.

He starts reading from the file and I compare the facts I have with the facts he has. The resulting story is chaos, with my sister swinging in on a rope like a pirate with a knife in her teeth, shouting some kind of crazy alien-language "YAWP!"

"And do you know what happened the day *before* the fight?" he asks, no longer reading from the file. In fact, he closes the file very deliberately.

"I don't think so." I gulp.

Turns out Jorie had a "confrontation" with a teacher in the library that ended when Jorie "threw a laptop" at her History teacher, which shocks me since she loved History class and was indifferent toward technology.

"Your sister threw a laptop at a teacher," he repeats for emphasis.

"Whose laptop?" I look toward the file, believing the answer to be in the manila container.

"It doesn't matter."

"Did it hit her?"

"This was assault, James. Your sister wanted to hit Mrs. Yao."

No one in school talked about this laptop assault. If it happened, why wouldn't they talk about it? The only thing people talked about was Gina Best's ambulance ride. Then the people who hate the pretty girls laughed about how Gina didn't really look all that messed up the next day. They listed all of Jorie's many transgressions, and assaulting Mrs. Yao didn't make the list.

I try to picture this scene. Mrs. Yao is a regular-looking teacher—not foreboding. Not the kind of face that is asking to get punched. (Unlike the gym teachers, who are all looking for trouble, if you ask me.) She doesn't have a reputation of any kind. Not one of the school favorites, but not known for hard grading or boring classes. Kids like her enough to not complain about her, which is usually the best thing teachers can ask for in a school with more than a thousand kids ready to tear the place apart at the first sign of a pop quiz.

"Is there any chance that what you're saying is not true?" I ask.

"There is *no chance* that it's *not true.*"

"Well, that double negative is not clearing things up."

I apologize once I see VanO's dour face.

"I'm sorry. It's not that I can't picture my sister losing it. It's just hard to believe she'd yell at someone who didn't deserve it. And I can't believe she'd throw a laptop at a teacher."

The vice principal considers me for a moment. I'm a nervous kid with inconsistent facial hair and no reputation except that Jorie's my sister. But he doesn't know about how I listened to all the one-sided fights Jorie lost at home. All the yelling and assaults she absorbed. Of course, she took out her anger on lamps, trinkets, doors, and walls, so my momentary image of her as a silent, suffering girl is inaccurate. But if VP VanO knew her life outside of the halls of this school, wouldn't he have to understand how she got to the breaking point? How all the little things became big things and all the big things became like a wildfire menacing everything flammable?

No, he wouldn't care. It wouldn't make a difference, because he'd say she deserved all the trouble.

"Mr. Whitman, I think you have too much faith in your sister. Because you don't deny that she beat up Gina. And you don't seem surprised."

"I was surprised. When it happened. Gina and Jorie used to be best friends," I say.

"*Used* to be."

Now VP VanO knows that I came in here to fight for my sister despite not knowing all the details of things she'd done. Who beats up her former best friend? Who throws a laptop? Especially one that works perfectly well?

The anxious vomiting butterflies wake with a burst. VanO keeps speaking, but the sounds aren't making their way down my ear canal. I see his mouth moving, and there are little darts of noise—words, I suspect—getting through. But I'm in a wet-lunged, lightheaded, heart-pounding anxiety attack.

Do you know what it's like to be very embarrassed? Even when whatever you've done is unknown to others? I'm talking about the feeling you get when you *will* be found out. Not the same as when you *are,* in fact, found out. This is what I feel like right now. Mostly, it manifests itself as a burning right beneath my skin.

Then there's the fear, right on the heels of the original anxiety, that I'm going to cry in here and VanO will go out to ask Mrs. Berry for some tissues and Mrs. Berry will tell Mrs. Hatch and she'll tell her daughter, who is popular enough to have about a dozen friends (mostly guys) to tell. And then I'll be the crybaby again, but this time I'll be the short bus crybaby, mocked by even the short bus kids.

All of this is in my head and I can't get around it. My eyes are drowning. I just want to defend my sister.

12.

THE REST OF THE DAY sludges along; all my energy gets sucked up by my dirty sponge of a brain. I sweat and pace in my room after dinner. I have trouble falling asleep, and when I finally do, I wake up sometime later just as I nearly crack my molars by dragging them against one another. My heart pounds hard enough to pump wet concrete.

Weird worries press down on me: Did I eat dinner? Did I leave my homework at school? Did everyone smell the rank T-shirt I wore in gym? Did I forget to say thank you to the lunch lady? Does my mother know I contemplate messy suicides? Does my father hate me because I yawp in the morning?

I fear that I have not noticed crucial details about my life—my parents' anniversary, my best friend's birthday, my sister's moments of kindness.

I try to read but can't focus. I hate all my music. I rearrange the various gargoyles on my bookshelf. I pile up books I hate or will never read. I sneeze because of the dust, and then my skin gets dry and I have a headache. The air is humid but I'm cold. I go sit on the toilet but nothing happens. The sound of the exhaust fan is inappropriate at this late hour. I consider jerking off but can't stop thinking about unattractive things.

I think about the shark that ate bad dreams, which I haven't seen in years, and become obsessed with finding it. I can't find it, but I *have* to find it. I become hyperfocused on the absence of that particular thing, a thing I need right now. I pull everything out of my closet and from under my bed.

Once my closet's innards have been retched onto the floor and the bed—all the strange objects kill me with little dust swords in my lungs—I give up.

I pick up a book about the circus that I read a million times as a little kid. I don't even have to open it—my brain already knows the pictures. I remember one image of the circus elephant, holding its foot up and smiling. Elephants don't smile, certainly not in the circus. I saw a video of an elephant trampling people at a circus. It just *had enough* and went mad and the reporter in the video couldn't explain it.

Well, anyone would go crazy and trample people out of desperation if prodded, whipped, and shipped around the country to parade under lights and hold up a massive foot to amuse people. How hard is that to understand? Anyone would go crazy suppressing their preference for rivers, for savannah life, for squirting themselves with water.

I wish I were an elephant, so I had something serious to be depressed about.

When my alarm goes off in the morning, I have no energy to celebrate myself or hug trees or even look any birds in the eye.

13.

DR. BIRD WANTS TO KNOW if I've had any panic attacks this week.

I say no.

Then I say yes because lying to Dr. Bird is impossible. When I'm lying, she tilts her head dramatically and stares me down.

"Sort of. Started in the vice principal's office."

Dr. Bird asks whether I made any progress.

I'm not sure of the question.

Dr. Bird asks me if bringing Jorie back is for my sister's benefit or mine. I tell her that it's for Jorie's benefit.

Dr. Bird raises and slowly tilts her head.

"Honest?"

"I think."

14.

MY DAD AND I eat dinner without Mom tonight. One of those together-alone feelings hits me. The worst thing to watch the Brute do: eat. Especially foods with gravies or sauces. He's not a slurper, but he chews with his mouth open and often ends up with food around his mouth. Why he's not more conscious of his eating manners befuddles me. Each night, when he's done eating, he pushes his plate away from his body. It's usually piled high with about seven used paper napkins, yet he still ends up with some dot of food on his cheek.

I offer to just make some mac and cheese, but he wants to order a pizza. This means we have to sit around and wait for it—not even the rather pleasant distraction of prepping food can save me from a conversation.

We manage to get through the topic of school; then randomly my father asks how Derek is doing.

"Fine. I guess. Why?" We're sitting at the kitchen table. Empty plates sit ready next to glasses with rapidly shrinking ice cubes.

"I knew a guy when I was your age who'd lost his dad. He'd lost his dad a little later than Derek. I wonder if you know how hard it might be for him."

"He's always been fine." I wiggle a fork, focusing on it with the same blank stare my father's directing at the junk mail.

"It's a lot of pressure to live without a dad, I think." He folds a couple of flyers up, tosses them into the recycling box from where he sits, and then crosses his arms. "It's pressure to live in a broken family of any kind."

"I don't think he thinks his family is broken. He's got his sisters and his mother." The truth is, I've never thought about this. My father makes a good point. "I think people adjust, you know? I think, with my broken arm, I don't have to adjust because my arm will get better, but if my arm had been removed, I would adjust."

"You'd miss your arm. Just like Derek misses his dad."

I wonder about this whole conversation. What's my father trying to do, make me feel superior for having a dad? Or make me feel crappy about not thinking about Derek? Is this about Jorie? Either way, my father's certainty about Derek's emotional state irritates me. He's my friend. If anyone gets to say how Derek feels about things, it's me.

Thank goodness for doorbells and pizza delivery and my father's inability to carry on a significant conversation when food enters the room, because I might've said I am a little jealous of Derek's father-free life.

15.

WHITMAN PASSED OFF LISTS of things as poetry. It makes for a tedious read sometimes, but I think I know why he did it: it totally shuts down the mind. Thus, I spend all morning cataloging things in classrooms and hallways. My anxieties take a back seat to unfettered words—no sentences, no strings of repetitive phrases. No worries about what I said and how I said it. Just *things.*

Many of the things he wrote about don't exist anymore. Well, wagon wheels and blacksmith hammers, sure—somewhere those things are still in use. But he talks about stuff that is just foreign. I mean, what's a "jour printer"? What are "the frisket and tympan"? And what the hell are "the etui of oculist's or aurist's instruments"?

So I look at stuff and consider whether it will become extinct in a hundred years. I even take some covert photos. Maybe I could write a poem about objects that will be extincted by technology:

Chalk.

Chalk dust.

The black blackboard.

The curly wire of the notebooks,

the scraggily edge of notebook pages,

the little bits of paper that used to hold the paper in

the notebook.

Notebooks.

The ink pen,

the gel pen.

Mr. Hobbelstein's aviator sunglasses.

Mr. Hobbelstein.

I'm not sure if Beth will publish this, but it's a start. Pictures and poems. It would take up all sorts of space in the literary journal. Mr. Hobbelstein might be annoyed. But I can call the poem "Gone in 2112." If he thinks he'll still be here, then it's his problem.

My cell phone vibrates. I check it covertly, fearing the wrath of Mr. Hobbelstein, who believes cell phones are the worst invention since television. I have a text message with a picture of where a tree limb meets the trunk.

I text back:

> I swear I see now that every thing
> has an eternal soul!
> The trees have, rooted in the
> ground. . . . The weeds of the sea
> have. . . . the animals.
> I like this shot. Send me more!

She replies:

> Last days with my phone. Can't
> afford it. Enjoy!

As I look away from the photo and out the classroom door, I see the person who might be able to confirm why Jorie freaked out and got expelled: Mrs. Yao.

I ask for the bathroom pass and follow her, trying to glean her mood by the way she walks the halls. I'm not sure if she is displaying normal behavior, but she doesn't look anyone in the eye. Some of my teachers go out of their way to be friendly. Mrs.

Yao is trying to stay invisible. I always notice weird things about teachers. I catch some of my male teachers looking at the girls. I catch teachers yawning. I overhear complaints. I notice when their deodorant fails. I can remember keeping track of my seventh grade teacher's eye blinks.

Mrs. Yao doesn't display any strange traits, but she does dress like an old lady. She is not an old lady, but her skirt looks like something my grandmother would have worn back in the eighties. Or something she would have wallpapered her bathroom with in the sixties. It's hard to believe that Mrs. Yao has a husband. I can't think of most of my teachers as being married. They seem so dull.

Mrs. Yao darts into her classroom and nearly smashes my face with the door. I suspect this is accidental, but who knows how far her desire to be invisible extends? Perhaps she's willing to knock a few students upside the head to keep people at a distance.

Still, she doesn't seem to recognize me when she sets her folders on her desk and notices me pushing the door open.

"Yes?"

"I'm not one of your students."

"Okay?"

"But I was wondering if I could talk to you."

The look of panic on Mrs. Yao's face cannot be described

with words. Just know that she seems to fear all the possible things I might want to reveal to her, and the fear creates wrinkles and darkness around her eyes.

"It's about my sister. Jorie. She was in your class until a few weeks ago."

"Jorie?" The fear lines disappear, but her face doesn't change otherwise.

"Yes. She got expelled. She was in a fight and that was probably the real reason. The last straw, or something, but I found out recently that she had a fight or something with you." I fidget a bit and step farther into the classroom. "I'm saying too much."

"You are speaking, but you are not saying anything." She gestures for me to sit.

I don't want to sit at a desk for this conversation. I need to feel like something other than a student, and there's nothing like a school desk to make one feel helpless and physically uncomfortable.

As a compromise, I put the bathroom pass on the desk chair and I lean against the desk.

"I guess I want to know what happened. I'm trying to make a case to have her reinstated here at school."

I notice that Mrs. Yao's eyes are quite expressive for a woman who didn't look where she's walking in the hallway.

"Jorie was failing my class but not for any good reason. She handed in homework half the time. She failed quizzes. She failed sections of tests. But she also aced tests. She always asked good questions and answered my more open-ended questions."

I smile. These are good details mixed with bad.

"But I think I got her on a bad day. I came into the library and she was arguing with some students." Mrs. Yao begins writing things on the board but doesn't continue talking.

"What was she arguing about?"

"The argument started before I arrived. I heard cursing and insults that aren't worth repeating."

Mrs. Yao has precise, neat chalkboard writing.

"I moved her away from the conflict," she continues. "I just had this sense that something bad would happen if she stayed there. I pulled her aside and asked her if she was okay. But then I made a mistake and brought up the performance issues. I asked her why she didn't seem to care as much as she used to. I asked her what was getting in the way of her success." She stops here, but there seems to be something else she wants to say.

"That's what set her off?" I ask.

"Maybe you know. It wasn't this class. It wasn't school. It wasn't even the fight in the library."

"I'm not sure I can fill in the details here." Maybe I'm just not willing to fill in the details. I want outside sources. I want someone to construct the truth. I want to know what Mrs. Yao suspects.

Mrs. Yao busies herself in an unconvincing fashion.

"I heard she threw a laptop at you," I say.

"No! That's not what happened, really. Who would say such a thing?"

"It's what I heard. That she threw a laptop at you."

She asks me my first name. I tell her, and then there's a pause. I feel my phone sitting in my pocket and think about trees. I picture Jorie in a room somewhere, texting pictures. Even she's being obscure. (Or opaque? I'm not sure what word I mean.)

"James. Your sister abuses herself. That is why she got mad at me." Another pause. A horrible, terrible pause. "The cuts on her arm? You didn't know about them?" Mrs. Yao looks at me. I want her to look at papers or out the window.

"Who cut her arm?"

"She cuts her own arm." Mrs. Yao's finger cuts repeatedly across her forearm, a safe illustration of the truth.

"Oh." I swallow. Little prickly pains march down the back of my throat. This happens when I am nervous or, sometimes, when I eat an apple.

"She tried to kill herself?" I ask.

"I asked her that. She did not like being asked."

I am lightheaded. Right before my eyes! All the things I've noticed about strangers! All the things I've missed about Jorie!

Kids start coming into Mrs. Yao's classroom. She gestures for me to move with her near the chalkboard and whispers, "I didn't report this to the principal, James. She got angry and yelled and she *knocked* my laptop onto the floor accidentally. She did not try to hurt me. Maybe I did wrong by prying then and there. Maybe my tactic was wrong."

I want to believe Mrs. Yao, because she seems too normal to lie. Maybe she can't care about her students because it will mean she gets too involved. She tried to care about Jorie and ended up with a broken laptop. And maybe she used to look kids in the eye in the hallway. And maybe now she only sees angry kids who don't want to be bothered.

I look her in the eye and say thanks. She might think I mean thanks for the information. But she might also know what I really mean.

16.

I SPEND MY ENTIRE WEEKEND in the park, photographing trees and trying to think all poetical. It's surprisingly easy for my brain, it seems. Or, at least, the things I think *seem* poetical. Maybe I just think in rants and rambles like Walt.

It's pretty hard to hold the camera with my broken arm, but I still manage to use six rolls of this expensive super color film Jorie bought me. Digital cameras seem like the best thing ever, but film cameras offer a pleasing and necessary mystery that depends on the delay between the shutter-click and getting my prints from the drugstore. Anticipation seems healthy.

At first I try to avoid man-made things in my pictures, but then I think about Whitman, and he had no problem with man-made things. He loved everything. So I photograph clouds and airplanes dragging themselves across the blue. I photograph a leaf flat on crackling-gray concrete. I photograph an earwig in the nooks of a maple tree. I photograph the power lines disappearing into the crinkling twig-fingers of a tree.

The drugstore gets my photos done in twenty minutes, and I tell the lady who rings me up that the turnaround time is amazing.

"Not much volume these days."

"That's too bad."

"We spent all sorts of money getting this machine in, and now it's collecting dust."

I don't have anything to say. The decay of drugstore photo developing machines is not really on my radar of concerns. Sadly, this woman seems to have taken it to heart.

Back home I spend the rest of my Sunday afternoon looking closely at my photos. I have lots of great tree pictures. Pretty abstract stuff. Trees in parts—limbs, leaf stems, bark textures. I start a pile of good pictures and a pile of rejects. There are more good ones than I expected.

Lying on my bed, I hold pictures up against my dull ceiling. I have a great shot of two branches coming together in a V. It looks all artsy.

What I begin to see is hard to describe, but the one limb in the picture in my hand sort of matches a limb in a shot from another roll. Different tree, different limbs, but they blend well.

I hold the seams together and look for other photos that fit. Soon I have a long, winding tree arm, some that branch off into a burst of tinier, leafed branches. Others that are as bare as my own arms.

A fizz of energy shoots through my body. I turn on my iPod and shuffle through my *Los Campesinos!* albums because they keep me moving, jumping, active. Movement tricks me into feeling happy. I get a roll of tape and I stand on my bed and try to keep the photos aligned as I tape them to my ceiling, though it's tough with my cast. I match tree trunks with other trunks and tape some of the shots of individual leaves next to branches. I start cutting out a leaf from one photo, but that feels like cheating, so I toss the scissors and the cut photo aside and get back to making my Frankenstein photo tree.

My ceiling comes alive! My ceiling tree has roots with knuckle-y bumps and a huge trunk with half a dozen types of bark and leaves in color, leaves that don't match but are now together on the same tree. I use some of the blurry shots and even put the huge earwig picture up; the alien bug looks ready to leap off the ceiling.

After three hours of intense, strange craftwork I lie back, my head dotted with sweat, my heart suddenly tired. I have completed some kind of manic moment and the result is a strange, twisted tree that I will cherish every waking morning.

Dr. Bird is so proud of me that she fluffs her feathers and taps her left foot four times, as if she's trying to balance on one clawed foot but can't.

My mother comes in my room as I stare up at the product of my mania and asks what I'm doing while also telling me to turn the music down.

"How are you going to get this to school?" she asks.

"What do you mean?"

"Did you do this for school?"

"I just did it." I hold out a stack of the photos I didn't use for the ceiling tree. "I had all these pictures and I wanted to look at them. I saw how some of the tree pieces fit together—the pictures fit together, I mean."

Then my father decides to poke his nose into something that I did not invite him to take part in. As such, I move toward my door, hoping to signal to both of them that entry requires that they show some respect for my artistic endeavor.

"How much money did you spend printing all these?" the Brute asks.

"It wasn't a waste."

He exhales. They leave, condescending me in their mean brains.

I put on a song and let it repeat seven times. But the song is grim and pushes me *down down down.*

I take a picture of the photo tree with my phone and e-mail it to Jorie's address, though who knows if she'll get it. Then there's more anticipation, the bad kind. I've sent out a little ping into the tube-ether of the Internet and imagine all the reasons that no response appears.

I wish I could call a girl like Beth to ask her about her Sunday and forget mine.

Instead, I go into Jorie's room looking for poems but also, maybe, perhaps looking for some evidence to refute or confirm what Mrs. Yao said about Jorie cutting herself.

I use some of the Banshee's invasive snooping techniques—I jab my arm between the mattress and boxspring. I look and feel under the bed. (Bad idea! Crumbs! Hair! Something that feels like peanut butter *that isn't peanut butter!*)

Her closet is a densely packed mishmash of clothes and boxes. Shoes, art supplies in plastic containers, old encyclopedias that she used to cut pictures out of.

In the back, behind a stack of comic books, I find a wooden box that's loosely tied shut with a black ribbon. I undo the bow and lift the lid. For some reason, this doesn't feel like an intrusion. Still, I look over my shoulder.

The box holds a bunch of white notebook pages with handwriting scratched in fine blue ink. I get scraps of words, but there are also dark lines that are not ink. It looks like maroon.

I'm not sure, but I think it's blood. What else would it be? Centered on each page is a large fishhook of blood. Or a *J*. Probably a *J*, but the curls at the base of the *J* are smeared on some, thin on others, thick on others. The written words do not intersect with the *J*s.

I read the pages. It's poetry but not. It's a story but not. It's memories and dreams but not. Is this what she was going to publish in the *Amalgam?* Did she plan to reveal the abuse? Bruises? Welts? The cutting? My father, the Brute? My mother, the Banshee? Me, the invisible boy?

Maybe. Jorie is writing about some version of herself in the book. Different name, different looks, but familiar arguments, familiar angers. The sentences are compact, fast, brutal. Reading this *is* an intrusion, but it reveals things that I need to know if I'm going to end her banishment.

The girl in the story-poems is cutting herself. She's not doing it to die. She's doing it for something else. This is the explanation that I understand:

> *The lines are thin enough to not exist. The lines are nothing and then appear in red. The lines are lines; the lines are dots. The sharp lines on my arm are made with a sharper line of a blade. Like meets like, even if it hurts for them to meet. The lines*

fade and I can recreate them anywhere. But I need to breathe easy while I do it. I need a steady hand. A straight thin line, not too long, makes me feel better. A curve hurts. A curve ruins the whole moment.

I have mastered lining myself with evidence.
The evidence has mastered invisibility.

I pick up the box lid to replace it but see that inside the lid are taped a dozen razorblades in a square around a quote:

This hour I tell things in confidence,
I might not tell everybody, but I will tell you.

I put the lid on quickly and hold it on the box for fear it might lift itself off and make me face the shining pain again.

For some sick reason I think that I could publish this. I could make her private pain public and then people would know that she wasn't just the girl who got expelled for sending someone to the hospital. She was a person in pain with no outlets.

But who would want to read it? Who would read it seriously? Who would feel better knowing that someone else was in so much pain that they hurt themselves to feel something different? I can't imagine Beth's face if she read this. It seems foreign—Beth wouldn't cut herself and probably would think Jorie is a freak.

Maybe Jorie *is* a freak. She's in exile, and that's what a freak is: someone who doesn't belong and who can't belong.

Here's the night she got kicked out. As I remember it.

Dinner, for me, was non-nutritious and eaten quickly. My parents used anger and fear as appetite suppressants.

At seven o'clock, my father got off the phone with the principal.

I was in my room. Godspeed You! Black Emperor murmured from my stereo. Their music half fades into the background when you're not listening, and I was not listening, and you never really know when the album is done and starting anew. It feeds into itself quite nicely.

The music was loud enough to mask the words but not the anger.

Despite three solid years of this kind of simmering anxiety followed by bursts of fighting, I still got a little shock in the lungs when I heard yelling.

One thing I had stopped doing: turning the volume down to hear the details. The details never came through clearly enough anyway. The Banshee would yell something about curfews. My sister would yell about clothes. The Brute would smash his palm against a wall. And often the fights would never really end. Or they never ended with words. There was plenty of yelling. Yelling, though, seems to negate the meaning of words.

Understand too that I am more familiar with the sound of my family's angry voices than their laughter.

So I was on my computer, doing some homework or downloading music while listening to music. I was in my pajamas. My room was cold because I shut the heat vents to cut down on the dry air. I get nosebleeds. It's intolerable. I wore socks to retain heat. My feet were pulled under my desk chair. I remember lots of pointless things about the way the night felt.

I heard little peaks of yelling over the peaks of music. I listened but I didn't listen.

But then there were sounds that didn't belong—*vicious* sounds. Alarming vibrations tendrilled through the house. Prolonged yells from my sister coming from downstairs. I should hear her running upstairs, slamming her door. I should hear pounding on her door. I should begin to hear the concluding yells as Jorie shuts down.

I muted the music and listened. I was afraid to get caught listening, but the sounds from outside my safe little room were loud, mixed up, unnerving. I heard glass break. I heard the

Banshee yell, "You are an embarrassment! I can never explain you to anyone!"

Jorie screamed something over and over.

I pressed my ear against my door and heard feet drumming up the staircase. I thought we'd gotten back on track. Jorie got to her room. My parents followed up the stairs. More yelling about respect and criminal charges and ambulances.

Then something huge crashed in Jorie's room. I pictured—for a quick, guilty moment—her pinned under her bookshelf. An accident, but one that could defuse the entire house immediately. Everyone will apologize. Everyone will get along.

I hadn't done this in a while, but I started to mutter a hope or maybe a prayer. I wanted this all to go away quickly and without comment.

"Don't touch me! Don't touch me! Don't fucking touch me!" Jorie screamed.

The hallway walls took a few shots from someone's fists. I should've opened the door to look, but I couldn't. I felt the doorknob in my hand, but it felt like Saturn—like a gas giant that would mist between my fingers.

THUMP

THUMP

THUMP

THUMP

THUMP

THUMP

THUMP

THUMP

Some of the thumps ignited a yelp of pain.

I looked out my door, and since the hallway was clear, I moved to the stairs. I peered around the corner and saw my father drag Jorie out the front door by her hair and her arm.

He's not a very strong man. Jorie's not a very strong girl. Their movements were jerky, vulgar. It's not the way bodies were supposed to move together. But there it was.

I saw all this happen. I saw Jorie sobbing on the front lawn. She tried to get up and stumbled. I expected her to run back inside the house or yell or something.

But there she was on the lawn.

And there I was, looking down as my father shut the front door and my mother bawled in the kitchen. All of them oblivious to my presence.

A better brother would have done something. Instead, I ran back to my room to continue being invisible. In a way, this was not a lie.

No one mentioned the episode until three nights later when I asked why Jorie wasn't at dinner.

"She's eating elsewhere," my mother said.

"From now on," my father said, a scratch on his face where a scratch never existed before.

After putting the box of secret pain back in Jorie's closet and fashioning a terrible bow, I go back to my room. The sweat of bad knowledge keeps me from pretending that I just have too much caffeine in my system or that I'm worried about schoolwork. I wish I had normal anxieties. I wish I had athletic skills so I had an outlet for all this mania in my blood.

I lie on my back.

I lie on my stomach.

I lie on my side.

My room is hot, but it's really me, or something inside of me, that cannot get cool. I can't slow my mind down. My head's all wrapped up in my stupid family.

I go on the Internet. Derek posted a video of a baby on its stomach that farts, letting loose a puff of baby powder. I note that this is funny but do not laugh. Otherwise, there are just stupid status wars and complaints about school projects.

I write Jorie thirteen and a half e-mails but only send the one that asks how she's doing, not the ones that admit I'm still doing nothing.

17.

IN THE MORNING, the ceiling tree greets me but doesn't seem as masterful. I contemplate it for a moment, and then my father's irritating knuckle-rap on my door stirs my anxieties.

"Get up."

"This is my barbaric yaaaawwwwwwwwp!"

"What?"

"I too am not a bit tamed, I too am untranslatable!"

"What the hell are you doing in there?"

"I'm up!" My attempt to irritate my dad has ended up irritating me as well. Go figure.

At school, Derek talks about his pizza shop job and how the middle school girls come in to giggle about his sideburns over shared drinks and reheated slices.

"Are you hiring?" A job might be exactly what I need.

"You need a job?"

"I need to be out of my house a bit more." This is the most I've ever admitted about my feelings.

"Do you have pizza shop experience?"

"I have eaten in them."

"That might be enough."

He smiles, but I don't know if he's serious or if I'm serious.

For most of the morning I am drowsy thanks to an entire weekend of insomnia and anxiety. This Monday feels worse than a Monday.

I run into Beth after lunch and tell her that even though Jorie said she didn't have anything, I snooped in her room again.

"Did you find anything?" she asks.

"I found something."

Her face glows.

"But we can't use it."

"Crapplejacks!"

There's a pathetic silence.

"What is it?" she asks.

"It's something that I think she wrote for you, for the *Amalgam.* I think it was supposed to be her . . . barbaric yawp."

"Like Whitman?" Beth curls her lip. It's clear she's not a fan, but at least she knows what I'm talking about.

I can't be sure if I know my sister's real intentions. It doesn't seem normal for someone to do something so private and then want to tell everyone. But as someone who thinks about suicide—particularly the thrill of who would find me and how guilty they'd feel—I guess there's always something public about secrets.

"Can I see it?" Beth asks.

"I'd like to let you, but I think it became more a private thing than a piece for the *Amalgam*. You know? It just felt like it was one thing and then became another."

I fully expect and prepare myself to accept that Beth will now no longer need to talk to me. Because, honestly, this is the only reason she said hi to me in the first place. To get Jorie's final piece.

Nanoseconds pass and I panic.

"I did have an idea." I hesitate—if I tell her about my ceiling tree she might dismiss me as the loser I feel like 94.5 percent of the time.

"Uh-huh?"

"I take photographs. I thought maybe I could write some poems that have photos to go with them."

"Like a photo-essay? Or a photo-poem, I guess?"

"Yeah!"

"We don't print on glossy. So the photos would look cruddy." She does this thing with her eyebrows and her lower lip that is too adorable to describe accurately. "Actually. There have been requests to publish artwork. Most of it is bad tattoo stuff. Line flowers with thorns. Comic book chicks. That kind of stuff. But it could be worth doing if you have photos."

"I can show you some of the photos. It's nature stuff, but I can do whatever."

"Yeah. Yeah! This might work." I can see her mind working.

"It's amazing to see someone who actually gets excited about stuff like this. Writing and art stuff."

"According to my parents, I started reading when I was, like, two years old. I love books and stories and poems. My friends only sort of tolerate it. I brought a book on a class trip once and my friends made fun of me. There aren't many people who would even think of putting photos and poems together for any reason other than maybe if they wanted to burn things. So, I feel like maybe you and I were meant to know each other!"

She smiles a smile I believe and then darts off to class before I can ruin it by saying something goofy.

18.

THE GLOW OF MY CONVERSATION with Beth doesn't fade. The malfunctioning parts of my brain try to find reasons to be discouraged, but the fact is that Beth sees me as someone special. Nothing more—yet—but nothing less.

Like Walt says:

I have perceived that to be with those I like is
enough,
To stop in company with the rest at evening is
enough,
To be surrounded by beautiful curious breathing
laughing flesh is enough,
To pass among them . . . . to touch any one . . . . to
rest my arm ever so lightly round

his or her neck for a moment . . . . what is

this then?

I do not ask any more delight . . . . I swim in it as in

a sea.

While in my reverie, I pass Gina Best in the hallway. I'm probably too confident, but I think I should talk to her. I should find out why Jorie beat her up (though rephrasing the question will be necessary if Gina is to tell me anything).

Gina Best doesn't look like she has fought or will ever fight anyone. She looks like she will be a broadcast journalism major and then a talk show host and then end up involved in a murder-suicide after cheating on her husband. She's tall and athletic—meaning her arms and legs are thick but not flabby. She's got big brown eyes and perfectly straight teeth and no sign of ever having dealt with braces or acne. Most people probably didn't even know that she and my sister were best friends way back in elementary school. Gina slept over at our house four weekends in a row once.

Gina and Jorie stopped hanging out with each other in eighth grade when Jorie got mono and stayed home from school for half the year. When she came back from her quarantine, Gina was best friends with someone else and they just never got back in line with each other. Jorie ended up listening to lots of hip indie music; Gina went with a crowd that loved hip-hop. There could have been a ton of other reasons, but that's what Jorie told me.

I skip three classes tracking Gina and working up the nerve to talk to her. I'm not worried about school at this stage. I'm worried about me and Jorie. I need us to be under the same roof again because if we're together we can help each other. All I confirm from following Gina around is that she smokes, has plenty of guy friends, and is what everyone would agree is gorgeous. Even though I spend the day staring at her back, I cannot deny that the way her body is crafted deserves an award. Whitman would say something about her hips and bosoms. Looking at Gina would make anyone think about the act of reproduction. And isn't that the point of the Ginas of the world? To make sure we keep on making more Ginas so people stay interested in making more Ginas?

Like Walt says:

> *Urge and urge and urge,*
> *Always the procreant urge of the world.*

Gina eats during a different lunch period than I do, but the mass of people makes it easy to blend in and watch her with her friends. It's all the kinds of people that reject Jorie. These girls are not poetry readers, not girls who cut themselves, not girls who would wear heavy metal band T-shirts or belch after chugging soda.

Or maybe they are. Who am I to say they're not?

Toward the end of lunch, Gina heads for the doors that lead to the courtyard, leaving her friends behind, so I catch up with her. This is yet another moment when I have no idea what I'm doing.

"Excuse me. Gina."

When Gina spins, her hair flips cinematically. She recognizes me and we both stand there quietly for a moment.

"What do you want?" she asks.

I come right out and ask her why Jorie beat her up.

"Because she's some kind of crazy person, clearly." Gina walks, I follow. She offers me a cigarette; I decline with a wave of my hand.

"I know that you guys haven't been friends for a long time—"

"That's not true," she says. "We've always been friends. I thought so, anyway. We just haven't been *best* friends. We just haven't hung out aside from in classes. I never hated your sister and she certainly had little reason to hate me."

"Oh."

Gina smokes without concerning herself with where the smoke ends up, which means I inhale far more than I'd like.

"I talked to the vice principal about the day of your fight," I say. "He said that the day before, Jorie got into an argument with Mrs. Yao and that she threw a laptop at her."

"Oh, yeah, I heard about that."

"Really?" I say. "Mrs. Yao didn't report the incident. To anyone."

I try to read Gina's face.

"Well, I heard about it," this marvel of bone structure and skin tone says. "I heard your sister freaked out in the library at some kids and then Mrs. Yao came over to break it up and then your sister threw a laptop at her or something."

"But that's not what Mrs. Yao says."

"Well, I didn't tell you about this, so why are you bothering me?" Gina inhales so hard on her cigarette that I can hear tiny tobacco leaves burning.

"I want to find out if there's a way to get her unexpelled."

"Not likely to happen, James. She sent me to the *hospital.*"

"What if you ask them to let her walk at graduation?"

"What am I supposed to do, go in there and plead with them to let her finish out the year? Give her another chance to cut my face up?" Gina presses her finger just under her tiny scar. I realize now that she has a tan and it's not summer yet. She once dyed her hair with bright blue Kool-Aid and let my sister pierce her ears with a safety pin.

"Look, you can believe me or not," Gina says, "but she started a fight with me."

I wish liars just revealed themselves with a glow that others could see. But they don't. And I don't have the ability to read faces or tics or beads of sweat.

"Jorie got kicked out of the house because of all this, Gina. Literally dragged and kicked out of the house."

"She's probably better off." She tosses her cigarette and pulls out her phone, dismissing me.

God! Everything she does is like from a movie. She's going to be famous. Strangers will weep over her murder-suicide!

19.

TONIGHT, DINNER WITH MY PARENTS is a jovial affair. We begin with classy appetizers including Havarti dill cheese on crackers and some Rumaki. We discuss the latest showings at the art galleries in the city and schedule an outing to the Ritzy Cinemas to see the latest French film. Our main course: lobster ravioli in a blush sauce. For dessert: tiramisu. We tell jokes, laugh. I impress my father with my wit and even recite some Whitman to celebrate the culinary delights:

This is the meal pleasantly set . . . . this is the meat
and drink for natural hunger,
It is for the wicked just the same as the
righteous . . . .

I ask for a glass of wine and receive it without lecture—I feel adult, accepted, in the right place and the right time for the first time.

Of course, our real dinner is nothing like this. I'm just trying to ignore the empty spot at the table across from me where Jorie used to sit and roll her eyes whenever something eye-roll-worthy was said. Such as when my mother talked about how badly she wanted to apply for *The Amazing Race* with Jorie.

"Think about how much closer we would be, Jorie—traveling together, working together, winning together!"

"We wouldn't win," Jorie would say.

"Of course we would! I think we would."

"I'm not sure a couple of Americans running around in foreign countries is something the world can handle," my father would grumble. "You'd be walking targets. I wouldn't be surprised if we found out that some of the people booted off the show were really kidnapped by terrorists." This was followed by a stern insertion of his fork into his mouth, and then: "Don't roll your eyes at me, Jorie. Show some respect for god's sake."

Tonight, I pick at my iceberg lettuce salad (nutritional content: none) and try to find some of the frozen cheese ravioli that have been cooked thoroughly enough to eat. (My mother mixes meat and cheese ravioli together; meat ravioli taste like the devil's nuts.)

"Has Jorie called or anything?" I ask.

My parents are silent. Just hearing the name of the banished irritates them. Or maybe they easily erased her from their minds.

"I thought she'd call. I haven't gotten an e-mail."

"She doesn't e-mail you?" the Brute asks. "Selfish."

It's like he's mad on my behalf and that makes us buddies.

My mother doesn't contribute to the conversation. My mother is like iceburg lettuce.

I carry around Jorie's secret box of pain in my mind. Images of her weeping, alone, cutting herself, haunt me as the school days progress. I hand in some homework, I fail some quizzes, I pass some tests. Everything averages out.

One night I get a permanent marker and color my entire cast a shimmering black. It's not black enough, though, and I feel like I should've done something more creative.

I ask Dr. Bird why I feel so depressed all the time.

Dr. Bird pecks at her wing and says I'm only as depressed as I feel.

"That's a little circular."

Dr. Bird trots in a circle.

"I've been taking pictures, but nothing comes out that good. I feel like I'm wasting money on film."

Dr. Bird says the world gets less compelling when I'm depressed, so I'm just seeing pictures in a negative light.

This makes sense but doesn't make me feel better.

I dismiss Dr. Bird and write Jorie an e-mail:

Jorie—Hey. I'm having one of those days. A day like all the others, I guess, but it's pretty thick and foggy here. I don't know what causes this stuff. I try to find outlets, but nothing seems to really defuse the anxiety except more depression. Does this make sense? I know you have similar issues. I know you had that therapist. Are you still seeing her? Is she expensive? I think I need to see someone. I'm not sure how to get through a day without anxiety or anything. I guess things aren't that bad. How are you? How is waitressing? Do you need anything?

Send me tree pictures.

Here's a quote from Whitman:

"The clock indicates the moment. . . . but what does eternity indicate?"

—James

I have one of those hours of just waiting at my computer and refreshing my inbox while checking my Facebook page. But she doesn't e-mail me back. Then I remember that she doesn't have a computer or a phone and now I'm not even sure when I'll see her again. I guess Derek can get in touch with her since his lady is Jorie's boss. Seems like a convoluted way to contact one's sibling.

After school the next day I have an e-mail from Jorie:

> James—My therapist's contact info is below. Good luck getting Mom and Dad to pay for it. I'm not sure if they're just cheap or hateful. I only got two months before they stopped paying.
>
> I attached a picture. I saw a leaf on the ground that was dried but still green. It curled in a bit like a dead bug. I broke it in my hand into pieces big and small. I took a picture of the pieces, close up. That's the picture. That's how I feel. Don't feel like me or maybe don't tell me you feel like me. It makes it worse.
>
> —Jorie

As you can imagine, the next few days involve vomiting stomach butterflies, although I've started to imagine them as moths because butterflies seem too delicate and pretty to puke.

I try writing a poem about it:

Dirt-colored paper wings that tear easily when I
swat.
Moths fly for my eyes, my mouth.
They want to be inside my stomach to flutter and
puke.
I want to hold them in my palm to watch them,
To find something pretty to say about
The things that wake my anxiety.

That might be passable. It's short, but I could see Beth printing it. She's faced with publishing suburban angst by the other editor, so she might as well publish my angsty moth poem.

After my depression refuses to disperse for days, I sit at breakfast with the words "I need to see a therapist" on the tip of my tongue. My mouth would prefer to ingest rather than express, though, so I end up eating four pancakes the size of my head. Large pancakes on a mothy stomach will make for a sick afternoon, but then I realize I'm in for a lifetime of sick afternoons if I don't speak up.

"Mom-I-want-to-see-a-therapist," I blurt.

She's at the counter putting dishes away. I think she heard me and is pretending she didn't hear me.

"Mom?"

"What did you say? The plates were making noise."

"I said I need to see a therapist."

"What for?" She asks this in a concerned voice, but it's concern for herself, not me. I'm very sure of this.

"I can't really explain. I feel broken."

"Well. Maybe you should talk to your father about this."

The words *father* and *dad* mean very specific things in my house.

When he gets back from one of his real estate lunches, he seems like he's in a good mood. Perhaps this is related to beer. Perhaps not. My grandfather's relationship with alcohol, the way my parents tell it, could fuel a number of TLC specials about abused wives, lost jobs, and angry children. Still, my father's anger never seems linked to alcohol—just to fatherhood.

I want to ambush my father with my request to go to therapy, but my mother ambushes me instead.

"James has something he needs to ask you." She stands there in the front hallway, the look on her face pleading with my father to just get through the conversation quickly. I can't tell if she wants to help or just erase my request from our family history.

Removing his jacket and shoes, he asks me what I need.

"I think I need to start seeing a therapist person."

His arms flop to his sides and his shoulders droop in an exaggerated manner.

"Uck. This again? What good did therapy do your sister?"

"Dale," my mother says.

"What? It's an honest question."

"This isn't about her," I urge, and that feels about 75 percent honest. "I have anxieties."

"Don't we all." The Brute sits down at the kitchen table with me. "Therapy isn't what you need. You just need to organize yourself. Figure out what you want to do in the world. College and work."

"I don't think that's it."

"No, it really is. You're just at that age where you think everything is so horrible and terrible."

My mother puts a glass of iced tea down for him. The glass seems to start sweating as soon as he touches it.

"Your father may be right, James."

"I think this is something more." I want to say "more serious," but they're both looking at me like I'm a spoiled brat. Maybe they're right. People in the world suffer from greater calamities than I do. I eat, I have clothes, I have a house. I read about people around the world who survive on less than a dollar a day. I read about how there are hundreds of millions of widows living in poverty. I see ads for kids who are born with ragged lips and jagged teeth. I don't have anything like that. I just wake up with a deep hatred of myself. How selfish is that?

"You guys are probably right," I admit.

"Of course we are. You're probably just getting ideas from Jorie. And look how that turned out."

This, though, is not excusable. I have four response options:

Get up, stomp up stairs, slam the door, ignore them when they begin banging on it.

Get up, go outside, climb a tree, and come home when we've all buried our emotions.

Get up, tell my father he is a tremendous prick, throw his iced tea across the room.

Get up, tell my mother she gave birth to fucked-up kids because she married a fucked-up man.

Despite all the options, I pick the quiet one involving trees because I am a coward with nothing to be sad about.

20.

DEREK GETS ME A JOB at the pizza shop and it's the kind of thing I guess everyone has to suffer through. Plus, I need money for therapy.

I come home reeking of grease, of all things. Not pizza, just grease. I have to put my work clothes in the washer immediately, otherwise the stench infects my entire room. Who knew pizza baked in such a horrible stench?

Because my arm is in a cast for a while longer, I'm just a register jockey who wipes down the booths with an old rag. All the other register people are girls. Derek says that most pizza shop owners hire teenage girls to run the register because they have a fetish for cute girls in T-shirts that smell like grease and wear their hair in ponytails.

"It's really one of the lesser-known fetishes," he says with a laugh as we take out the garbage one night.

"Are there websites?"

"Probably. But they're all in Italian so you'd have to look up '*adolescente pizza grasso ragazze*' on Google."

"Seems like too much effort."

The job pays me under the table, a concept that had to be explained to me a couple of times. I can't grasp the concept of an entire pizza place that officially pays no employees. Is the IRS that stupid?

When I tasted the pizza I realized that they probably didn't make enough money to attract any attention. How is it that in this day and age a pizza place can exist and make terrible pizza? Seriously, if you put ketchup on cardboard and barely melted some store-brand cheese you'll be more satisfied because at least then you wouldn't have dropped ten bucks.

But what do I care, really? I need a hundred bucks a week for therapy sessions that my parents won't pay for and won't know about.

Whitman would love this pizza shop. Everyone reeks of labor even though only two of the seven employees really work (I do not include myself in this list of workers, please note).

Whitman would say something like:

Look! The stained shirts,

the hands that knead themselves into the dough,

shaping a world

from yeast and water and flour!

These five young men standing by the hot oven

sweat

the sweat of generations,

the recipes, the love, the burdens!

He did not write this, but narrating the world like Walt Whitman makes me smile. Even when it comes out sounding homoerotic.

As I'm Whitmanizing and wiping down an orange booth, the doorbell tinkles and in walks Beth with three other girls I recognize but immediately ignore.

"Hey!" I say. I haven't told her I've become Pizza Boy, but what does it matter? Do I even have a chance to win her away from her boyfriend? Can girls get over the smell of grease?

"I didn't know you worked here," she says, and her friends furrow their brows (I've stopped ignoring them since they're clearly judging me).

"I need a little cash." I want to tell her why. She'll understand, or at least tell me she understands. But confessing the need for mental health services in a pizza shop in front of three judgmental girls and my boss seems ill-advised.

Beth and her friends move to sit at the booth I've just wiped down, but I shoo them into one that isn't damp. (Of course, the booth-cleaning rag gets rinsed out maybe three times a day, so the other booths, while dry, are probably dirtier.)

They order a pizza and I hang out behind the counter looking busy. I want to talk to Beth but not to her friends. They smile secret smiles. I do my best to eavesdrop, hearing things that could be innuendos but could also be about a thousand other things in the world.

As I bring out the pizza, I fear the fingers on my broken arm are too weak to hold the tray. Beth will end up with eighth-degree burns and years of skin grafts. I sweat in fear from this unreality, making an accident more likely.

In reality, I get the pizza down fine and even get a thank-you from nameless girl number two when I drop off a stack of extra napkins.

"Here you are, ladies. Pizza is messy no matter how proper the people eating it." I smile.

Beth laughs and the other girls laugh a nanosecond later, suggesting that they are laughing at her and maybe me, but definitely her.

I offer to get refills and then flee.

Back by the oven, Flip, the owner, asks me to read a receipt to him.

"It says, 'Philly steak onions peppers provolone.'"

He nods as if I confirmed what he already knew, but I suspect he can't read words he's seen a hundred times. Who can't recognize 'Philly steak' when someone orders it every day?

"What's with the girls out there?" Flip asks.

"How do you mean?"

"You know them?"

"From school."

Flip looks over at them as I wait for some kind of skeevy comment—something about extra sausage on their pizza or a more direct "I wonder if they want to have sex in my van?" Instead, he tells me to charge them for everything or I'll get fired.

"No comping! I fire people who give their friends free food." He goes away and I'm left by the hot oven hoping that Beth will leave before I say something stupid. But then I peep around the corner and see her standing at the counter. Her friends are cleaning up and shuffling outside.

"What's up?" I ask her. I'm trying not to be weird.

"Hey. That was good pizza."

"The extra flavor is from not washing my hands." I wiggle my fingers at her.

Beth laughs. She's at ease now that her friends are outside.

"I've been thinking about your photo-poem," she says a bit rapidly. "I'm *really* into the idea, so I hope you were serious."

"I am rarely serious, but I was serious about that."

"Good. You just—I get this sense about you that you're really observant. But not that you pay attention and take good notes or something. I feel like you really see things that other people don't see and that you think about things that other people ignore."

My face is hot enough to warm up a slice of pizza. I don't know how to respond to such a compliment.

I think I say thanks, but I would need outside confirmation to be sure.

"So are you saving for a car or something?" she asks, deftly shifting the conversation.

"Nothing that cool."

"Talk to Jorie at all? Since the party?"

"She's fine." I feel like a traitor of sorts. Why am I lying about the state of my world? Can't I be honest? Can't I tell her that I hug trees and wonder about ways to kill myself?

"That's good." She turns to look out the door. "I gotta go. It was great seeing you!"

Beth looks like she wants to tell me more great things about me.

Or maybe I'm just projecting.

I'm probably projecting. I'm a projector.

For example: The world is not terrible. I just keep thinking it is.

21.

I ASK DEREK ON FRIDAY if he can take me out to the restaurant where his lady, Sally, works with my sister.

He hesitates.

"If not, it's cool," I offer.

"It's just that I'm going out with her when she gets off work."

I prepare for some kind of crude comment about the sexual adventure they will embark upon in the parking lot.

"I mean, if Jorie's there," I say, "I can hang with her and figure out a way to get home later."

"I can find out if your sister is working and if you promise you can find a way back home, I'll give you a ride." Derek raps his knuckle on lockers as we walk to lunch.

My anxiety over finding a way to get to Jorie for a visit disappears. Anxiety over finding transportation home erupts. (Jorie has no car and I've never been on a public bus before.)

"Also," Derek says, "I need you to do me a favor."

"Oh, dear. Your favors."

"Don't be a dick. I'm staying at her condo this weekend and I told my parents I was sleeping over at your house. So cover for me."

This sounds like a demand, not a favor.

"You haven't slept over my house since sixth grade, dude," I say.

"Just do it, all right?" He looks around, then whispers, "She wants to have sex with me in the shower!"

"Then you'd better get some waterproof condoms."

The confused look on his face is beautiful.

On Friday, Derek confirms that my sister is working, so he picks me up at seven-thirty. We recite jokes along with an Aziz Ansari CD, though it's getting a little old since we do that a lot. I track how long it takes to get to Fillmore's and notice that while there are a few Plexiglas bus stops, they are all unlit. Clearly the kind of place where teenagers are mugged, raped, mutilated, and murdered. I might end up running home, screaming like a twelve-year-old girl.

The restaurant is packed. The hostess seems to know Derek.

Perhaps he's met Sally here a few times already, which would be stupid considering she's engaged. I guess visiting your engaged restaurant shift supervisor girlfriend at her place of employment doesn't seem like a bad idea in Derek World. But who am I to judge? I haven't been out of the house two weekends in a row since I was born.

Derek sits up at the bar, acting like he owns the place. He head-nods to the bartender. We get sodas. I try to figure out what all the little buttons on the soda hose do. It occupies my mind while my eyes scan the crowd for Jorie.

At eight, Derek's lady comes over. She's done with her shift, doing all those little things food service people seem to do when they've just finished a long shift: hair tussling, back stretching, sighing.

I expect them to hug or even for her to touch him on the back or arm, but she's all professional-friendly. You would think they were cousins or friends, not a seventeen-year-old boy and a twenty-one-year-old woman living out a strange romance.

"Say, I never asked you," Derek's lady says, "what happened to your arm?"

"Oh. It got caught in a cotton gin."

Derek and I laugh, but then she asks what a cotton gin is and I just admit I'm kidding.

"He got hit by the short bus."

"Oh my god!" she says.

"It was kind of embarrassing."

"No kidding," Derek says. He's not devoted to making me feel terrible, though. "Actually, he was saving an injured bird."

"That's so sweet! Who would risk themselves for something like that?"

"Yeah. I mean, thanks."

I feel good.

Sally goes to her car and Derek lingers behind for a moment to see if I'll be all right.

"Remember, I'm sleeping at your house, so if for some insane reason my mom talks to your mom— "

"Yeah, man, go have a swinging good weekend."

"You'll be okay getting home?"

"I'll figure something out."

Derek leaves me at the bar with a brotherly shoulder punch. I tell him not to get his lady pregnant.

After fifteen seconds I realize I'm a sixteen-year-old kid taking up a barstool, so I ask the hostess for a table or booth in my sister's section.

Jorie is halfway through her "Welcome to Fillmore's" greeting when she realizes it's me.

"What the hell are you doing here?" Her voice is tired but happy.

“Surprise?”

She sits across from me for a second but then looks around and gets back up.

“Don’t want to get fired. They don’t like us sitting with customers.”

“Even family?”

“Especially.” She taps a pen against her forearm. I can’t help but wonder if the skin of her arm has been marred recently.

“How are you?” I ask.

“Good. Tired. Are you here with someone? A date?” She looks hopeful, like she wants to be the cool older sister, but I disappoint her.

“Derek dropped me off. I thought we could talk for a bit. Not trying to get you in trouble.”

She says she’s off at ten and then has plans to go to a party that I can come to.

“It’s not a crazy thing. Just some friends. Good people. They’ll like you.”

I have some money that’s supposed to go toward my therapy. Instead, I get cheese fries, drink three huge sodas, and plan to give the rest as a tip, leaving me with no bus fare. I don’t even know how much a bus costs, but I definitely won’t have enough.

As the last hour of Jorie’s shift passes she drops off plates of random crap: burnt onions, celery sticks, gummy bears, peas. I build an island for the gummy bears with a celery slide.

At ten, Jorie comes over and falls into the seat across from me. I feel numb and overwhelmed after sitting in one place killing time, basically trying to shoot smiles her way to help her through.

"You look beat," I say.

Jorie looks down at her shirt and holds part of it out for me to inspect.

"How did I get this?"

"Is that steak sauce?"

"Or the blood of that unruly birthday boy."

"Did stabbing him affect your tip?"

We laugh and head outside to walk to her apartment, which she says is about ten minutes away. I tell her it's a convenient location and think that maybe she's doing okay until I see the place. She rents the upstairs of garage.

"I know, it's a shithole," Jorie says while shouldering open the door. "The worst part is that there's flying ants or termites or something."

There aren't any noticeable bugs when we walk in, but it could be because it's dark.

The apartment is essentially one big room—there's a mattress on the floor with rumpled blankets. The kitchen has blood-red cabinets and black and white floor tiles. It looks like a 1950s diner where customers routinely get stabbed. There's a sort of living room area, though Jorie has no TV, no couch, no table, and only two cruddy-looking used floor lamps like the kind that my mom always said would catch fire and burn the whole damn house down.

Jorie and I used to play a game, inspired by my mother's constant stories about her childhood, called Poor Kids. Basically, we'd spend the day in our backyard and pretend to eat roots and grubs, sew our own clothes, and collect dirty water from an imaginary well. Jorie liked to be the hunter, which was fine with me since I always liked to pretend to cook. (My specialty: mudburgers cooked in the sun on a piece of slate.)

This apartment makes me feel like Jorie is playing games again.

Jorie changes in the bathroom and I worry about this party and my curfew and wonder if termites are eating their way through the last bit of wood holding everything together.

"There might be something to drink in the fridge," she yells from the bathroom.

I open the fridge and see three cans of whipped cream and a bowl of what looks like cake mix.

Jorie comes up and peeks in.

"I didn't have any food except for a cake mix. I tried to make it with just water, but it tasted like shit. Needs eggs and oil." She laughs.

"At least you have whipped cream, right?"

"My friend Mike brought that over to do whip-its."

"What's that, like a drink?"

"If you inhale the gas in the can it fucks you up. I hate it. I felt like I was falling through the floor."

"Can't that kill you?"

"I wasn't actually falling through the floor."

"No, the gas."

"Oh. Yeah, that can definitely kill you."

Two dudes pick us up; they seem nice enough. They even turn down the radio so that we can all talk. Jorie tells them that I'm a reader and good in school.

"Yeah, I'm a big nerd."

"Nothing wrong with that," the dude driving says. "I wish I did better in school. I wouldn't have to install ventilation systems."

The other dude says the money's good, and they start talking about people they work with. I hear them but don't listen.

The party is at some house rented by seven people that may or may not have known each other since elementary school.

It's hard to follow the conversations because of competing radios, conversations, and a guy trying to impress people with an out-of-tune acoustic guitar.

I am the youngest person in the house. I am the youngest person on earth. I follow Jorie around, trying not to sit next to her for fear her friends will think I'm lame, but I stay in the same room, taking up corners or sitting squished on couches. I drink a beer to buzz away my butterflies. If I drink too much I might forget to go home.

Someone passes me a clay pipe. I ask what it is because I think it might be rude to just pass it along, but asking what it is seems like a stupid thing to do. No one laughs, though. These people are so nice!

"It's sticky icky, icky, icky!" someone says in a high-pitched voice.

"You are not hip enough to pull off that line," someone else teases.

Before I can even pass the pipe along, Jorie jumps up and takes it from me.

"Dudes! Not my brother."

"I was just being neighborly," the guy says.

"It's all right," I say. "I can just say no."

The room erupts in laughter, except for Jorie. I realize too late that I sounded like one of those terrible anti-drug posters in the gym teacher's office. She laughs sarcastically and goes to another room. I stay on the couch and try to disappear completely.

Long after my curfew, Jorie finds someone to give us both a ride home. I think the guy's name is Dutch. Or Hutch. It's got an "utch" sound.

Jorie sits in the front seat. I'm nervous; Utch seems very high. I want to be cool and not embarrass my sister, who has gone out of her way to make me comfortable all night, even after I accidentally made everyone laugh at her. Seems like I'm always guilty of something that ends with Jorie being punished.

"Holy shit," Utch giggles, "was that purple thing a *dinosaur?*"

"What?" Jorie says.

"It was a purple rhinodactylus! One of those flying things!"

"What the hell are you talking about?"

Utch is looking over his shoulder at me.

"Did you see it?"

"I didn't." If I had seen a flying purple thing, I would be very, very frightened. As it stands, the fact that the guy driving saw it should frighten me more.

The car is going very slow and we're sticking to back roads. Jorie navigates and Utch keeps talking about seeing things.

"Are you tripping?" Jorie whispers.

"I can hear you," I say.

"I'm way past tripping," Utch says.

I can hear the things my father would say about this. *This is what you do with your time? This is the way you choose to live your lives? This is the smartest decision you can make—get a ride home from the highest guy at the party?*

"Go slowly," Jorie says. "Don't kill me and my brother."

I want to have faith that nothing will happen. Whitman would say that I should have faith in the universe. I can't think of any lines relevant to this situation.

Then Utch drives into a parked car.

After a moment, I get out of the back seat. Jorie gets out of the front seat. There's steam or smoke or an angry car spirit misting from the front of Utch's car.

"You should get out of here, James," Jorie says.

"Should we leave him?"

"No. You should go. Cops will be here. You don't need to be here."

I look at Jorie and she's wilted. Her night will never end. I wonder if all her nights have been like this since she got kicked out.

We go over to help Utch out, but he waves us off. The driver's side door makes a magnificent crunching sound as it opens. I look at the dark and crackled windshield. The streetlight or the moon reflects in it. I want to take a picture, which seems stupid, but there it is.

"Did I kill it?" Utch says.

"What?"

"The rhinodactylus!" He has a giggle fit and then sees blood on his hands and gets quiet.

Jorie pulls me away and urges me to leave. She points me to Batch Road, which I can follow all the way back home. I start walking and listen for the sounds of cops, but the night is quiet except for Jorie reading her friend the riot act.

22.

WHEN I GET HOME there's a note on the front door that reads: "This is entirely too late."

It's my mother's handwriting.

I open the door quietly and head upstairs. Pictures of my mother and father line the upstairs hallway. Other relatives are peppered here as well, but the constant inclusion of my youthful parents has always suggested to me a strange vanity. Hold on to youth, ignore life with kids. My parents do not seem emotional in the pictures; they mostly embody verbs—they blow out birthday candles, they raise hands in the air along with a crowd of others, they shield their eyes from sun, they throw Frisbees, they barbecue. Even in shots of them hugging or smiling, I sense no real emotion. Maybe I can't see them as people; maybe they will always be malfunctioning robotic parenting units.

I'm about to open my bedroom door when the Brute's voice shotguns the back of my head.

"Who told you *this* was okay?"

I turn around and whisper, "What?"

"It's two-thirty in the morning."

"Sorry."

"You pissed off your mother."

I want to say that he's going to wake her up, pissing her off more, but decide not to push it.

"Sorry."

"I don't want sorry. I want to know where you've been."

"Out with Derek."

Oh, shit. Derek is supposed to be sleeping here!

"Really. How come he didn't drop you off?"

"He did. Up the street. I didn't want his car to wake you up."

"Don't lie."

Clearly I've already forgotten Rule Number One of Teenage Happiness: *Less detail makes for an easier lie.*

My father stands in the hallway, crosses his arms. He's very alert for two-thirty. And he's using a voice he only ever used with Jorie.

"I was out with Jorie," I admit.

"Great. Were you drinking?"

I sigh, dramatically and angrily.

"And who said you could hang out with her?"

"No one."

"Exactly."

"I didn't know I'm forbidden from seeing my sister."

My father, the Brute, walks toward me and I fear the health of my other arm. If he touches me I will freak. I can feel the freakout in my throat.

He just walks past me to the bathroom and rips a fart that would have made me cackle when I was little.

23.

IN PHYSICS ON MONDAY, Beth pretends like she doesn't know me. I try to figure out what I did wrong. Maybe it's because I work at a pizza shop. Maybe the idea of it—along with the smell—makes her too good for me. I don't blame her for thinking this, but I just want confirmation. Confirmation would let me move on without staring at her and out the window at the same time.

After school I go to Mr. Pines's classroom, where the *Amalgam* has its meetings. To be honest, I walk past the door four times, peering in casually to see if there's anyone there. But I can't tell. I hear voices, but none of them sounds like Beth's.

I take a deep breath and close my eyes. I'm standing a little ways down the hall and a few people are still walking around, but I don't care if they wonder about the guy with the all-black arm cast holding his breath and shutting his eyes.

I consider running outside to find a tree to feel the comfort in a hug, but finding a tree that lets me wrap my arms around it *just so* will take time and attract attention.

I let my breath out. Two cheerleaders walk by me slowly, staring at me without worry. It must be nice to find the world strange but to keep walking.

The lit mag editorial team looks at me as I enter and drop my book bag by the door. I wave with my broken arm—basically I flash my arm at them, sideways, signaling that I am friendly and unarmed. Ha-ha.

"What are you doing here?" Beth pops her head up from a laptop and smiles. Perhaps she's not harboring some kind of grudge.

"Thought I'd see where the famous literary magazine got put together."

I dig out a CD from my bag and walk over to offer it to these self-appointed gods of the high school literary scene.

"Also, I have some photos and poems. Like we talked about."

One of the guys by the laptop asks what's on the disc.

"An idea. Nothing definite," I say cryptically. I notice Beth's concerned face. Maybe she hasn't broached the subject of a multimedia, Whitman-influenced poetry extravaganza.

"James takes great photos, Roy," Beth says, snatching the disc from the co-editor. "I wanted to see them. I have an idea for a special end-of-the-year issue."

"What's the idea?" Roy's curiosity and annoyance seem equal.

Beth starts explaining her idea of a visual issue, poems and pictures, and the three other students seem into it until the co-editor pisses all over it.

"And how are we going to print color photos in a black-and-white publication? Did you consider that?"

I want to defend Beth from this sophomore whose poetry I've never read but would definitely hate.

But Beth does fine.

"We put it on the school website, *Roy*. Save all the printing money to throw an end-of-year launch party."

I'm surprised. She's really into this idea.

"Can we do that?" Roy asks.

"Of course we can! Don't you think Pines and the department would be thrilled to save a little money going forward? We could do the whole magazine online next year."

"We could even make an app for people's phones like *The New Yorker* or something," another kid suggests. Roy rolls his eyes, but Beth stays quiet. She doesn't want to oversell it. (I don't blame her. I can't imagine kids downloading a school literary magazine to their phones. They won't even pick it up in classrooms for free.)

Beth loads the disc. The photos appear on the screen of what I assume is not a school laptop since it looks expensive and has stickers all over the back.

I stand there as strangers and Beth evaluate my work. Though I don't consider it work—it's just twenty photos I scanned in the library.

"I like the colors," one person says.

"I notice colors and textures a lot," I say quietly. "Trees have good textures."

Roy doesn't say anything. I get the sense that if he were controlling the laptop he'd be clicking through the images much more rapidly than Beth. But she's giving me a great showing. By the end it seems like everyone has a favorite. One girl asks to see an image again and begins to analyze the balance, talking about the rule of thirds or something that sounds really technical. She asks me if I've ever taken a photography class and when I say I haven't she says I have a natural eye.

"That's funny, because I actually have robot eyes," I joke, and the girl looks confused, but at least Beth laughs.

I tell them that there are some poems that can go along with the images, but not many.

"Well, we have a little time to sort everything out." Beth

gives her team some work to do and Roy just concurs with her orders and suddenly it's just me and Beth sitting at a different desk on a different laptop, reading through bad poems. Together, alone.

"I've been weird," she says.

"What line is that?" I think she's reading from the poem on the screen.

"No. I mean *me. I've* been weird. I've wanted to talk to you but e-mail seemed like the wrong way."

"Are you breaking up with me?"

I smile.

She does not.

"You know when I came by the pizza shop with my friends?"

Ugh. I do smell of pizzeria.

"I had made the mistake of telling one of my friends about you. They said from the way I liked you that I talked about you. I mean, the way I *talked* about you that I *liked* you." She blushes. "They were teasing me about you and then they teased me in front of my boyfriend and then my boyfriend freaked out."

"I'm so sorry." But really I'm sort of not sorry, because I think Beth likes me in a way that messes up her words, which means it's not just about poetry and friendship.

"You didn't do anything," she says.

"That's . . . true."

"Anyway, Martin freaked out. And I freaked out at my friends. So I've been weird about you now."

I'm not sure what to say, so I start reading the bad poem on the screen. It's from someone lamenting the loss of love, written by a ninth-grader. I wonder if the feelings are real.

"This is a bad poem," I say.

"Don't say that so loud. It's Jen's." Beth gestures over to the other computer. I think Jen heard us, but who knows. She doesn't look like she's had her heart broken recently.

"Sorry."

"Great, now my literary magazine staff will turn on me." Still, she's smiling.

"Have I ruined your life?" I ask.

"No. Everything can be fixed."

24.

AT THE PIZZERIA THAT NIGHT, I'm distracted. Images of Beth and the sensual summer we might spend together blast through my racing brain. I feel synapses sparkling.

I sing the body electric!

I can't remember what Whitman writes after that, but I know that he's singing of the synapses. He read books about the electrical pulses that the body uses to communicate. He wasn't just invoking metaphor. He was invoking *science itself.* What a genius!

Flip tells me to wipe the tables down, and as I smear the gray rag around I try to tell him about Whitman and how our bodies are electric. Flip actually seems interested until the phone rings and he goes off to make a pizza. I rummage through my bag under the counter and pull out my tattered Whitman anthology.

This is the female form,
A divine nimbus exhales from it from head to foot,
It attracts with fierce undeniable attraction,
I am drawn by its breath as if I were no more than
a helpless vapor, all falls aside but myself . . .

I think that's erotic. Right?

People come in to pick up their orders and I take their money. I want to tell them the pizza is terrible, but some of them are regulars. Plus, I don't care! Let them have what they want! Maybe they like the pizza! Maybe the chewy cheese pleases them! Maybe it's all they want at the end of a long day! Who am I to say what pizza people should eat? I should take their money with a grin and wish them a good evening! I shouldn't judge their pineapple and pepperoni combos! I shouldn't *tsk-tsk* their extra sausage! I shouldn't judge the obese who come in wearing old running shorts and stained Phillies shirts and flip-flops! I shouldn't judge the frazzled mothers who can't corral their kids! I shouldn't judge the men in suits who eat a slice with their ties flipped over their shoulders! I should embrace them all!

That's the line that follows *I sing the body electric,* ringing loud from my memory: *The armies of those I love engirth me, and I engirth them.*

I'm not sure if this is what I feel, but it's a Monday night and I'm full of energy. Let me celebrate something other than myself for once. Let me celebrate the fact that a girl might like me and her boyfriend might be jealous of me and her friends might make fun of her for even wanting to be near me but she told me all this anyway!

Derek comes in and I can't wait to tell him about my day.

"Flip!" Derek yells.

"What?" Flip yells back.

"You screwed up that last order! It was *no* onions. You put on *extra.*"

Flip comes out with a slip of paper and holds it up. Derek and I both look at it. "Cheesesteak peppers onions."

"Yeah. Well, you put on extra onions and there was supposed to be no onions."

"Why would I write *onions* if someone didn't want onions. There aren't onions *by default.* You don't have to ask for *no* onions. You have to ask *for* onions. So they must have asked for onions."

"They asked for no onions."

"According to who?"

"According to them! So I'm out a tip and they didn't pay and now we have a bag of onions." Derek tosses a bag on my freshly wiped down counter. Sure enough, when I look inside there are just a ton of soggy, brownish onions that Derek apparently had to remove with his own hands.

"They didn't pay and you only brought back the onions?" Flip is outraged. He goes off to make a pizza. It's the way he gets rid of stress.

I tell Derek that I had a great moment with Beth.

"A moment?"

"Yeah. More than a moment, but there was a moment that was very important, I think."

"Did she touch you where you pee?" he asks.

"Metaphorically."

"I'm not even sure how that happens."

"She told me that she liked me. And her friends made fun of her for it. And her boyfriend found out!"

"That all sounds pretty awful, actually."

"No! It's great!"

"For you but not her."

"She said I didn't ruin her life." I feel like I'm bouncing up and down but I'm actually standing still. My heart's racing.

"Well, that's a good way to start a relationship: 'Hey, I didn't ruin your life. Let's date!'"

Derek's not trying to make me feel bad, but he's not really seeing the great part of this whole thing.

"Flip, what do you think?" I walk over to where he stands by the pizza counter, which is stained with pizza sauce, smashed vegetables, and meat drippings.

"What?" Flip asks.

"There's this girl and I thought she hated me but it's not that at all."

"It's nice when girls end up not hating you."

"Yeah. She's got a boyfriend. *He* hates me. But she's into me."

"You dog!" Flip accidentally knocks a metal container of cheese on the floor.

Before I can even get the broom and dustpan to him, he's swept most of the cheese back into the container with his hands.

"You want me to toss that out?"

"Eh. Most of it didn't hit the ground."

Flip must think that the layer of cheese that hit the ground first prevented contamination of the rest.

"Anyway," he says, "is this girl going to dump her boyfriend for you?"

"I don't know."

Derek says it's not likely.

"Why not?" I ask.

"Girls don't dump one guy for another guy."

Flip says they do. For the first time in my life I'm inclined to believe Flip, but I quickly back off as I watch him lick a piece of floor cheese from the heel of his hand.

"Derek," I say, "can you tell me why you know this?"

"Look, Sally and I have been going at it for two months. She hasn't even mentioned breaking off her engagement."

"Who's Sally?" Flip asks.

"My lady."

"Doesn't anyone date a girl who isn't already dating something else?" he yells.

"Flip." Derek puts his hand on Flip's shoulder. "You have to go where you're wanted. I can't help it if Sally is already engaged."

"A man doesn't stick his sausage in another man's pizza!" Flip declares without irony.

Derek and I burst out laughing.

"That's classic!" I declare.

Derek gets a call on his cell and goes outside to take it.

I tell Flip that I didn't mean to get involved with this girl.

"It's not even really a romance or anything. We just like being around each other. And I'm writing poems for her literary magazine."

"Poems for a girl? That's not romance?"

"No! The poems aren't for her. Really."

"Look me in the eye and swear that you aren't trying to impress her with your poetry."

When Flip says this it makes my whole life sound so stupid. Like I'm some loser back in England trying to woo one of the queen's handmaidens with sonnets about her bosom. And yet I'm doing it in the style of a gay poet *whom she doesn't even like.*

I don't answer.

"Exactly," he says. "Do me a favor. If you steal this girl away from her boyfriend, don't tell me about it. I've lost two wives. So it doesn't make me glad to hear that this is the way things work with young people."

Flip goes off to smoke a cigarette.

Derek comes back in and starts cursing before I can even recognize that he's upset.

"What's the matter?" I ask.

"You fucked me!"

"What?"

"My mom ran into your mom at the bank. My mom said she hoped I wasn't a bother this weekend!"

Fuck.

"What happened?" he yells.

"Well, I can't help that our moms ran into each other for the first time in months!"

"Your mom said you were grounded because you were out seeing your sister. That means I couldn't even say that you and I went to a party and that I ended up somewhere else. You totally messed this up for me!"

All my gleeful energy melts out of my feet. My stomach is cold and this grim tightness wraps around my torso.

"If she finds out about me and Sally I am *royally screwed.*"

"I didn't tell my parents anything about that. They don't know where Jorie works. It's fine. It's fine!"

"It's not fine!"

"Derek, it wouldn't have mattered. You weren't at my house. My mom would have said so regardless of me being grounded or not."

Derek doesn't seem convinced.

Flip comes back in and, one conversation behind, yells: "And how are you two getting girls that don't mind you smelling like pizza?"

25.

HALFWAY THROUGH MY FIRST therapy session I begin to hate the sound of my own voice. Or maybe not the voice but the words. Or maybe the way I'm saying the words. That would be my voice, I guess.

My therapist looks like Lady Gaga's mother. I'm not sure if that's exactly accurate—who knows what celebrities' parents really look like when the celebrities themselves don't look like real people. But around the eyes she looks like Lady Gaga. So, there it is.

Her name is Dr. Boesche but she says to call her Dr. Dora. I spend the first ten minutes talking about Jorie. Nothing specific about her banishment, but a little about her apartment and her friends. I feel like I need to urge Dr. Dora to worry about Jorie so she'll call my sister and give her free therapy or something.

"James, why don't we talk about you today? I can't really

help your sister since she's not here. And I can't talk to you about anything Jorie and I talked about."

"Okay. Sorry."

"Don't worry. Lots of people don't know what to talk about when they start therapy."

"I know what I want to talk about, but I don't know how to . . . get to it." I laugh.

"Just say it."

"I think I have mental health issues."

"Uh-huh. And?"

"I think my mental health issues are preventing me from being happy."

"You're talking around what you want to say. And in here you have to commit to saying exactly what you think and exactly what you feel. It will make things much easier."

"I usually do this with a bird," I admit.

This clearly throws Dr. Dora for a loop.

"I imagine that I have a bird therapist. A pigeon. And I don't have to express what I'm thinking to her since she's part of my brain."

Dr. Dora is not taking notes, so she must think I'm a lunatic.

"Which makes me a birdbrain," I add, hoping to win her over.

"And how long have you imagined a bird therapist?"

"About a year, but I've talked to her every day since Jorie got kicked out."

Dr. Dora asks me a few questions and I try to answer honestly, but there are things that I don't want to say out loud. I don't want to admit what I know about Jorie and her cutting. I don't want to admit to interfering with Beth's relationship because a) Dr. Dora will probably think I'm a bad person, and b) she'll probably tell me that being in a relationship is a bad idea if I have mental health issues.

"What do you do for fun, James?" Dr. Dora leans back. It's almost like she's asking me on a date. She puts her pen down, even. I don't find her attractive, but now I feel like I should.

"I work at a pizza shop. I guess that kills my free time."

"Do you play sports? Watch movies? Read?"

"I read. And I like movies. I'm not athletic, though."

"What do you read?"

I blank on most of the recent books I've read and liked. She's going to judge my choices, so I have to be sure I tell her things that will make her think I'm worth helping. If I tell her things I've never admitted—like how I read *The Story of O* and a bunch of Anne Rice erotica at the county library and jerked off in the restroom—she'll think I'm a pervert and will report me to my parents.

And the librarians.

"I like Walt Whitman. Mostly, that's what I go back to. I even carry a copy around with me."

"What do you like about Walt Whitman?"

I think and think. Is it one thing or everything? I begin to chill and panic. Anxiety attack number four thousand twenty-six approaches.

"I read him in college," Dr. Dora admits. "So I know a bit about him."

"I can recite parts." I say this to be impressive but laugh, too, because I'm nervous.

"That's good. Memorizing poems is more fun than saying you work at a pizzeria."

"I guess I like him because he says everything. And he thinks everything has something good about it. And even when he gets depressed about the Civil War or when his mother died—you can see some of the darkness in the poems, but ultimately he always comes back to sing."

Talking about Whitman lets me talk about how I broke my arm and my anxiety attacks.

"Do you feel anxious often?"

"Not really. A few times a month maybe. Lately a few times a week. Or all the time, I guess."

I have not admitted I have panic attacks to anyone. Derek

doesn't know. Jorie only knows that I've had a few bad days recently. Beth thinks I'm weird but not enough to dislike me.

My eyes water a bit.

"Do you feel depressed?"

"Who doesn't?" I laugh. I feel terribly sad. Like I'm hopeless, even though I've got a professional here to help me.

"I'm going to make a rule for you. You tend to laugh when you say things that are serious. I want you to stop doing that. Not just in here but everywhere."

"I'm sorry."

"Don't apologize for things that aren't your fault. Just be conscious of laughing." She asks me why I think I laugh.

"I never even noticed it."

"You need to start noticing it and stop doing it. You're trying to make serious things seem not serious."

"Okay."

"Do you think about suicide?"

I nod because I can't use my mouth to betray myself anymore. I want to say not a lot, but that doesn't seem true or helpful.

Dr. Dora writes a few things. She tells me to track my anxiety attacks and to write poetry about them if that helps.

"But there are some things you can do to help when you have an attack."

She tells me to breathe deeply, and while she's trying to show me how to meditate—something I thought a therapist would laugh at—I blurt out that I hug trees.

"Really? And does that help?"

"Sometimes." I start crying.

She asks me why I'm upset and I tell her that it hasn't helped.

"But, James, you're alive!" She finally seems like a person. "And you're here for help. Not everyone can get through these things alone."

I cry more. Too much for a guy. Too much for me to ever stop. I think about how I'm going to let my sister down because I'm not strong enough to help her. How am I supposed to be there for her when I can't hold myself together?

Dr. Dora lets me cry. I blow my nose with the thin, dry tissues next to my chair. I sneeze from the dust. These tissues are either cheap or not used much.

"I'm going to say something," she says. "It's too early for you and me to know for sure if it's necessary, but we're going to talk about this eventually. We might need medication to help you with the anxiety. But I'm not sure yet. It's just worth mentioning now to give you a sense of how serious I take what you've told me. How do you feel about that?"

"I don't want to be medicated."

"There are definitely things we can talk about to help you with your anxiety—things that aren't medicine. But I want you to be open to everything. I'm not the kind of person who will just throw pills at you and send you back into the world."

At the end of my first fifty minutes, she gives me her card and says I can call if I'm feeling very depressed.

"Anytime. It's better to call me than to not call because you don't think you're depressed enough."

"Okay."

"Promise."

"Okay."

"No, *say* 'I promise.'"

"I promise."

I apologize for having to pay in cash that smells like pizza and laugh a bit.

"There. Again. You have to stop that."

I almost apologize for screwing up, but then I say, "It may take me a bit to stop myself from laughing."

26.

THAT NIGHT I START AN E-MAIL to Jorie to tell her about therapy. Then I scrap the e-mail completely, realizing I'm more likely to see my sister in person than she is likely to get to a library to check her e-mail. How did people stay in touch before the Internet?

Dr. Bird says, "Messenger pigeons are efficient and whimsical." I think she's joking.

I stare up at my tree collage in low lamplight. I should be doing homework. I have two papers to write and a book to read and chapter questions to answer. I'm not sure what subjects go with what assignments, but I'm not convinced it matters. I'll talk my way into an extension for everything that's important and I'll take the zeros for homework. It's easier that way. Or maybe I just won't hand anything in.

I shut my eyes. Dr. Bird says she knows about my real therapist. Of course she knows. She knows everything.

"I'm sorry, Dr. Bird. I need someone who can think outside of me."

Dr. Bird asks what I think about medicating my anxieties away.

I stare at her round, black eye. I notice the shimmer to her feather color that looks like the gasoline rainbow in parking lot puddles.

I tell her I'm afraid that I'll become a muted person. Different. Dull. Like I'll be in limbo, constantly. I say I'm not sure if being numb is any different than what I feel now.

She asks me if I do feel numb. If numbness really captures what I feel when I'm anxious or sad.

"I can't tell right now because I don't feel like I'm anxious or sad."

She asks if I'm happy or calm.

"I feel like this is the kind of calm I can achieve."

I think about taking medication and then go online to read about the effects. Dr. Dora didn't name any medicines I should take, so I look up info about anxiety and depression pills. All the top Google hits are stories about kids who take antidepressants and end up more depressed and kill themselves. *The medicine made him do it.* That's the title to an article I don't want to read. Maybe it's just isolated cases that people are freaking out about.

Maybe the medicine doesn't make these kids more depressed, maybe it just didn't make them feel better and they gave up. Medicine failure, broken promise, last shred of hope. Goodbye.

I call Jorie's cell number just in case she got it working again. It rings and rings, so I listen to the rings for a while.

She is so much more damaged than I ever thought. Am I that damaged? I don't have a box of pain. I have a tree on my ceiling, though. I don't cut myself, but I hug trees. I spend more than a few nanoseconds a day wondering what it would be like to kill myself. Is this all the same thing but different?

I pull up Beth's contact information on my phone. I haven't called her before. Ever. But she gave me her number so we could text. I stare at her number and my thumb hovers over it, ready to initiate the call.

A warm feeling bubbles in my throat. I try to think about how I will explain a late-ish call on a school night. I try to think of what to talk about that's not scary and emotional.

Maybe I should just go downstairs and talk to my parents about nonsense.

Maybe I should call Derek and see how he's doing.

But I don't. I press the call button and somewhere in the sky, waves and radiation work to connect us. We live in the same town, go to the same school, have breathed the same air, laughed at the same jokes, but I'm asking for a signal to go to space and back to connect us.

Weird. I wonder if Whitman ever thought it was weird for people to use a telephone?

"Hello?"

I croak out a hello or something and my name.

"Hey, James. What's up?"

"Nothing."

And the sound of nothing follows.

I can't even fake a conversation in the state I'm in.

"I was thinking about something for the literary journal," she thankfully says. "What if we designed the journal with some cool HTML stuff so that your poems could float over the photos in different places and the reader can, like, click when they want the next line? It would be kind of interactive."

I'm willing to think anything is cool as long as I'm not talking.

"I can have my uncle do the work," she says. "He loves doing Web stuff."

"I think that would be really fun."

"You sound tired."

"Did I tell you I have a bunch of photos of trees on the ceiling above my bed? It's hard to explain. It's branches and roots and trunks and leaves. But I put it all together to look like one tree made up of many trees."

"That sounds really cool."

"It's hard to describe, but I'd like you to see it."

Yes, America, I just invited her to lie on my bed to look at my ceiling. A smoother pickup line has never been uttered.

"Hey, maybe we can even do *that* for the issue. Have like four or five of your poems and you click on different parts of a tree to get to it? That would be totally in line with Whitman, too, right?"

I hold the phone up to see if I'm actually on a call with someone real. I press a thumb against my left eye to check if I'm awake. The tests reveal the truth—that I'm having a small, good moment that I should cherish.

"That's a great idea, Beth."

"I think it would get more people to actually pay attention to the lit mag and to your poems, too. Just for the novelty of the Web presentation."

We stop talking and the silence is comfortable. It could be a golden silence. In fact, it is.

27.

AT THE PIZZERIA on a slow Sunday night, I ask Derek if he can drive me over to my sister's or to Fillmore's this week.

"I have to ask her something important," I stress.

"Just call her."

"No phone. I told you that."

"I'm not tracking your sister's life, you know."

Derek is texting furiously. I've never seen him so focused.

"Who are you texting?"

"Sally. Her fiancé found my jacket."

"Uh-oh."

"Well, it's not really my jacket. She got it for me and hadn't given it to me yet. But it was in their townhouse. He's a Mets fan, so seeing a Phillies jacket made him instantly suspicious."

"I can't believe you are screwing around with an engaged chick who buys you *official team merchandise.*"

"I'm very charming," but he says this without charm. It seems like things are weighing on him. At least he's not still mad about the weekend cover story mishap.

"You all right?" I realize, as I ask this, that I rarely ask him this. He asks *me* if I'm okay. He's asked me that pretty often since Jorie left. But I never inquire about him. I just assume he's happy because he's Derek. I've never thought of him as having an internal monologue. He gets mad, riled up, tired, worried, happy, hyper. But depressed? Morose? Introspective? Never!

"I'm just not sure about this whole thing," he says. "Sally seems to think this can go on forever—that she'll get married but we will keep messing around."

Sally's fiancé is a trainer for the Fillmore's restaurant chain, which requires him to travel all over the country to help train staff at various locations. He apparently will go away for months at a time. I ask Derek how people can be in a relationship like that and the two of us stare off in the distance, thinking for a good minute before we agree that marriage makes no sense anyway.

"Are you gonna break it off with her?"

"Not until I finish my sexual Jedi training."

Normally Derek would deliver this line with crude gusto, but he's staring at his phone like he just got a sext from Justin Bieber.

"So can you bring me over to see Jorie?"

"I don't think so," he says. "I just got a text from Sally that doesn't seem to be for me."

He holds the phone up to me and I see the message:

> Can't wait to see if you live up to the hype this Friday! See you at Fillmore's at 6:30!

It's followed by three smiley faces.

"I assume she wouldn't be talking to you about your hype?" In my head, Dr. Dora warns me not to joke about serious things.

"Is she cheating on me?"

This is not a rhetorical question. Derek wants me to confirm or deny his suspicions. My gut says, Sure, of course she's cheating. She's cheating with you on her fiancé. Why wouldn't she also cheat on you with someone else?

I resist honesty through sarcasm and choose ambiguous emotional support.

"I don't know, Derek. This could be a bunch of things."

"But this message wasn't meant for me. We don't have plans Friday."

"No. No, I would say it's definitely a mistake that she sent it to you. She's probably texting a couple of people at the same time. You do it all the time. But three smiley faces doesn't mean anything. And Fillmore's isn't exactly a romantic spot to rendezvous—I mean. Um."

Flip comes out with a well-timed delivery; I'm saved but feel bad for Derek anyway. I haven't been embroiled in a double-agent, older woman love affair before. It must be a whole new level of emotional turmoil and gratification.

28.

MY CAST FINALLY COMES OFF and my arm looks pale and thin and smells, but I think it helps me get over myself. At least something seems different these days.

Beth and I work on the lit mag website design after school. I try really hard to just relax and have fun and it takes me a few days to realize that I am, in fact, relaxing and having fun. Dr. Dora and Dr. Bird would be so proud of me.

That and I stop thinking about Beth as *a girl I like who might like me* and focus on how we have a mutual goal—to make the online literary magazine all sorts of crazy awesome.

For a week I don't think about medication or depression. I don't write anything in my anxiety journal because nothing I feel feels like anxiety. It feels like fun.

Her co-editor, Roy, gets into the website too, and the three of us end up staying on a Thursday until six o'clock. One of the maintenance guys comes by and tells us we have to leave.

"I'm not even sure why you're doing this here," he says. "You all got laptops. Go home!"

Roy tries to explain about the network storage and the website, but the guy clearly doesn't care.

As we're walking outside, Roy says he's actually really excited about the website.

"I don't even think my stuff is good enough for it. I'm going to try drawing, like, a short graphic story or something." He talks about an idea that Beth and I both agree will be great, and I feel good about Roy and his idea and don't even care if his skills fail to match his ambition. He's excited about something. It's infectious.

Beth sees her mom's car. Roy sees his dad's minivan. I see no car for me.

"Do you want me to wait with you?" she asks.

Roy waves and leaves without offering a ride. Maybe he knows what I'm hoping. Even though I've been relaxed about Beth and the potential for us to fall in love, even for just a little while, I won't deny that I have spent many moments staring off into space with the thought of a first Beth kiss. Does it make me seem like a liar? To say that I've been relaxed and focused on just the lit mag when I'm hyperconscious of the moves we'd need to make, to tilt our heads just slightly, for our lips to part just a bit, for us to move our faces close, casually, naturally, not like we're floating across space hoping to intersect, but that the gravity of our bodies, the gravity of our personalities, the gravity of fate itself, will bring us together in a kiss that will send tickles of joy through our lips, cheeks, faces, down into our hearts and beyond? Do you think this makes me an overthinker? A dreamer? Like someone who might loaf and contemplate a spear of grass?

Well, who cares, right?

I guess I care, because kissing this girl in front of the school while her mom sits in a car a few yards away would not be very romantic.

"It's all right," I utter. "My dad will be here soon."

We have a moment. I'm sure of it. It's a moment because we don't say anything and I think—I'm pretty sure—that Beth wants to hug me, at the very least, and then she does. It lasts billions of nanoseconds and I feel like I could blow up into a thousand happy pieces!

In the time after Beth leaves, I wait and think of all the stupid things I've hated about life before. It seems unreal that I would ever be depressed. How stupid it seems to hate life, to hate homework, to hate my parents, to get annoyed with Derek, to think I have any excuse to be depressed. What is there to be sad about when the world has possibilities? When even in the smallest spear of grass there is wonder?

My father's car pulls up. I get in and the stench of leather seats and a thousand cups of coffee and four thousand cigarettes engulfs me. I cough.

"Thanks for getting me."

"Your mother hates driving over here." He turns out onto the road that will lead to another road that will lead us over the highway and to our house. I hate being in the car with my father usually, but I'm feeling pretty damn good right now.

"You working tonight?" he asks.

"Nope."

Some awkward conversation follows. School and then work and then school again.

Then I think of something to push my luck in every sphere of my life.

"Can you give me a ride tomorrow night?"

"Where?"

"To Fillmore's."

"When?"

"Around seven?"

"Why?"

"I have a date."

My father and I have never discussed women before.

Women as in *women.* I got no sex talk. When I turned twelve I did find a strangely conspicuous *Family Health Manual* on my bed. The book, copyright 1968, taught me a few things about the dangers of masturbation and how girls spend their adolescence thinking about their periods. The Internet, copyright 2013, has refuted most of that book's basic claims.

"Who is she?"

"Thanks for assuming I'm straight," I tease.

"Ugh. Don't even joke. All that gay Whitman probably stunted your development."

My father has read no Whitman, as far as I know.

"She's a girl from school. We work on the literary magazine together."

"So she likes poetry?"

"She likes me. And poetry."

My father thinks. Using my excellent peripheral vision, I study him. Who knows what happens in his brain. He's probably wondering if he can sell her some commercial real estate.

"You'd like her, though, because she doesn't like Whitman." I need to charm my dad because, technically, I'm grounded. But maybe the prospect of a date will help more than charm.

He laughs the laugh he uses for me and my mom—a puff of air out of his throat.

"Here's hoping she likes Emily Dickinson," my father says.

"I don't get it."

"*Dick*-inson?" He sighs but smiles.

I guess I'm waiting for him to ruin my day. And here he is making a crude joke that Derek would have made.

Maybe that's the problem. Maybe my father just can't talk to me and I can't talk to him. Maybe we speak in different languages about things, and maybe it's too late for either one of us to try to learn a new way to talk. It doesn't help that I hate him for everything he's done to Jorie. But maybe he just didn't ever figure out how to talk.

"Do you ever get anxious, Dad?"

"Before a big pitch or an important lunch. Yes. But you know that to be successful you have to learn to hold that all in check."

"How do you do that?"

"It's different for everyone."

"No, I mean how do *you* do it? What works?"

He thinks. I start to think that he's making all this up—that he doesn't really get anxious.

"I think about something that makes me calm."

"What makes you calm?"

"It's personal."

I get a little pissed.

"And if I tell you it won't work. If I say it out loud it won't calm me. It has to be like that."

And that's it. We're back at the house and he's out of the car. No lecture about getting organized. No more jokes. Just that vague wisdom and out of the car. I should be happy to have even that much. I am happy that he didn't ruin my day. And maybe I didn't ruin his.

29.

I SCARF DOWN A BOX of macaroni and cheese with some broccoli mixed in and retreat to my room. I need to call and ask Beth out on the date that I told my father I already have. It would be devastating to my fragile reputation if I ended up having to cancel the whole thing.

The trick is, of course, that a date is only a third of the reason I'm going to Fillmore's. I need to talk to Jorie about Gina and see if I can figure out what is going on with this mysterious library argument. Plus, I want to spy on Sally to see if Derek should be worried about the guy we're referring to as The Hype.

I call Beth but get her voice mail. I leave a message that's brief and doesn't say anything. Just a hi-call-me-back kind of thing. But I can't wait for her to call me back. So I call again fifteen minutes later. Then I wait an hour. Call again. Then ten minutes. I don't leave a message each time because that would make me seem psychotic.

All the missed calls, though. Hmm.

I call two more times before I give up and just assume I'll see her at school and can ask her then. But what if she's making plans *as I sit here?*

Wait—she's got a boyfriend. They have plans. Why wouldn't they? Friday night? Young and in love? Of course—no. I shut my eyes and breathe slowly. I'm not going to let myself get all out of whack.

I sit up and feel the anxiety sweat bead out all over my body. I have to stop this or I'll be up all night predicting doom for myself.

I bought a panic attack journal. Plain green with a gold design. It looks like it's trying to be regal. The pages are lined, which I thought would help keep me organized. I haven't written in it yet, but tonight seems like the night to ruin the pages with my thoughts.

It's hard to know what to write, so I write: I'm anxious but not depressed. It's worry; it's worry about nameless things. It's worry about embarrassment. It's worry about letting people down for things that they don't even know I'm supposed to do for them. I'm going to write terrible poems for the lit mag. I didn't stand up for Jorie and I won't be able to get her back to school or back home.

The journal has quickly become a way to reinforce anxiety. After many rough attempts, I find this poem inside me:

It is too hot for crickets
and the wind has been blowing harder;
the remnant of some storm has come east,
less angry but still upset.

The trees lean into one another
like drunk men walking home
to wring out.

Their branches like bodies
twisted in sheets in a humid bed.
I listen for the continuation of rain
in the rumbling sound the heavy clouds make
as they drag their load somewhere else.

My pen falls out of my hand. I consider ripping the page out and throwing it away, but the poem is just a mood I'm in, not a confession. I close the book and lay it aside and fall back on my bed.

I press my palms against my temples and breathe. What did Dr. Dora say? I can call her but not for this. This is just a panic attack.

The trees. The trees.

I look up at my ceiling and breathe. I try to imagine each picture as part of its original whole and also part of the whole of the tree on the ceiling. Each picture has multiple dimensions. Or multiple existences.

Is this helping?

When I stop breathing and try to come back into the moment to see if the anxiety is receding, I lose control and get anxious.

Fuck! Fucking fuck!

I hate being this way! There's no way to stop it. It's my whole body acting against me. My body and my head—they want me to fail and stay locked in my room.

If I had more money I'd have gone to a second therapy session, but I won't go again because it's not worth the money or the time. Dr. Dora sucks.

I could go outside and hug a tree. But what will the neighbors say? My parents? The bats that flutter in our backyard some nights? Before I sabotage my only real active therapeutic option, I go outside.

I walk in the yard barefoot. The grass is icy but soft. I want to loaf in it.

I go back, deep into our yard, and see an oak tree. I go up to the tree that has preexisted me and might outlive me. I press my arms around the trunk and feel the bites against my inner arms. I itch all over my skin and I think about anxiety and medication and worry about losing myself or sinking further into this kind of stupid behavior. I can't keep going like this.

My phone vibrates in my pocket. I let it go. It might be Jorie or Beth or Derek or my parents. It might be government, watching me on a satellite. But I just want to stay like this.

It keeps vibrating; I can't ignore it.

"Hello?" I say.

"James?"

"Yes."

"Are you okay? It's Beth. You called a bunch of times."

"I'm in my yard hugging a tree." I think about what my father said and realize that I might just have killed the usefulness of this calming technique.

"Really?"

"I'm hugging a tree because I have panic attacks."

"I didn't know that."

"I have panic attacks and I get depressed. I'm not sure what the problem is."

Beth asks if I'm okay again.

"All I know is that I want to be okay, but I can't even do simple things that other people do."

"Why are you having a panic attack right now?"

Beth sounds like she is concerned. She sounds like she wants to help me.

"I wanted to ask you on a date."

"I gave you a panic attack?"

"I'm sorry. I didn't mean to make it sound like that."

"No, no! It makes a girl feel pretty special."

Is she smiling? Can I hear this girl's smile over the phone line?

"I'm sorry," I say.

"Don't apologize! Tell me what would make you feel better."

"Say you'll have mozzarella sticks and soda with me. Say you don't even have to think about it. Say you'll go with me even if you never thought you would eat mozzarella sticks with a guy who hugs trees."

"Yes."

"Yes?"

"Yes!"

Yes!

30.

I REALIZE I'VE COMPLICATED MY LIFE quite a bit. A date with Beth, questions for Jorie, fact-finding for Derek. Plus, yet another Friday night that I'm not in my room or pacing the house or fleeing out back to hug a tree. It's a whole new world. What would Whitman say?

> *I do not know what is untried and afterward,*
> *But I know it is sure and alive, and sufficient.*

Or something like that.

I get ready for this date like it's the only date I'll ever have. I shower though I haven't raised a stink. I shave though I shaved yesterday and my face does not yet demand daily shaves. I consider wearing a Life Is Good baseball cap but then figure I should put some effort in and do my hair. I have a tube of barely used gel. I try to make my hair look like Johnny Depp's—a bit of casual whisking of hair across my forehead. My hair's not long enough to go all Justin Beiber and it's a bit too thin to look like the *Twilight* guy. I'm not sure these examples will even appeal to Beth.

My mom comes up and asks me if I need a shirt ironed.

"No, Mom." She looks like she needs something to do. My parents think this is my first date. I guess it doesn't count if you meet someone down the beach and then make out against the fence around a mini-golf course.

"Is my hair okay?" I ask to make her feel needed.

"Well." She considers it. I have no idea if my mom even knows what cool hair is supposed to look like. Inviting her to even comment could be disastrous, because if she does something stupid with it and I change it, her feelings will be hurt. And if she does something cool with it I'll never stop thinking about how my mommy had to do my hair.

Am I going to be able to kiss Beth with a mommy-approved haircut?

She actually doesn't do much, yet I feel a little better about the mess of hair that I normally ignore.

"So, is this girl someone in your classes? Your father wouldn't tell me much."

"She runs the literary magazine."

"Interesting! She's a reader, then? I always knew you'd fall in love with a reader."

"It's not love, Mom. We're going to Fillmore's."

"You know what I mean."

I think about all the things my mother could mean about knowing whom I'll fall in love with. Has she always known this? Has my mother spent her life thinking about my future when I can barely think about my present? It must be terrible to be so hopeful and to wait to see if your hopes and predictions come true.

I think about Jorie and her secret box of pain and the fact that I hug trees and talk to a fake bird therapist and secretly see a real therapist behind my parents' backs. Did my parents think of any of that? Did my mom raise me to be the kid that gets hit by a bus trying to save a bird? Did she and my father think for even a second that it was kind of cool that they raised someone who cared enough about an injured animal to risk his life in the road to save it?

For some reason I assume that my parents are embarrassed by me. Rather than being *not what they wanted,* I'm just *not what they expected.*

"Mom?"

"Yes?"

"Can I ask something kind of important?" Fearing she might jump to a conclusion, I stress that it's not about my date.

"What is it?"

"I've been trying to get Jorie back into school. I haven't told anyone. But I've tried to get the vice principal to reconsider her expulsion. Do you think if I can do that, she could come live here again?"

I'm earnest, calm, hopeful. My mother's face is all worry. Perhaps the great anxieties of the world pass down genetically. I picture my father hiding his secret to being calm and my mother hiding her anxieties.

"That's up to your father."

"I feel like he'll say no unless you say yes."

"I'm not sure Jorie will want to come home."

"Let's say I can get her back into school. Just for the last month or so. So she can graduate."

"Is this something she wants?"

"I haven't told her yet. But I think it would be good for her to just finish school the way everyone else does. Counting down the days. Sitting through a long boring speech."

I could tell my mother that Jorie's life sucks, that her friends seem nice but irresponsible, that her apartment has flying ants, that her job runs her ragged.

I don't, however, reveal any of that or the secret box of pain or how she can't afford therapy but needs it, desperately.

"I'll think about it, James."

In my mind I hope all the chaos and anger my mother feels about Jorie will be ignored. I hope that my mother's apparent respect for me will help.

In the car, my father doesn't say anything.

When he pulls in the parking lot, he curses all the cars.

"Thank god we're not coming here for dinner. We'd never get a parking space. Jesus."

"I might have to bribe the hostess to get a table," I say.

"You need any money?"

Normally I refuse help from my father because it usually comes with stern instructions, lectures, fake wisdom, and the knowledge that he's the villain of Jorie's life and maybe mine. But a few extra bucks never hurts.

"I could use some. Just in case."

Despite his offer, my father begrudgingly gives me twenty dollars from his wallet. He probably drops more money on strangers.

I resist the urge to increase my anxiety further by mentioning Jorie. Hopefully my mom will talk to him.

"Have fun tonight," he says. "When do you need to be picked up?"

"I'll call." I wave my phone.

"Not too late. I have an early morning meeting."

"I might get a ride back with Derek. He knows some people here."

My father drives off.

Inside, I ask the hostess for a table for two in Jorie's section. Beth isn't here yet, but I figure the wait will be long.

"Jorie isn't here, actually," the hostess says.

"She always works Fridays."

"She actually doesn't work here anymore."

"Since when?"

"I think a few days ago? I don't know."

A waiter pushes the hostess aside so he can grab a stack of thick menus. She curses him and he huffs out an apology.

"What happened?" I ask.

"I really don't know; I'm really busy." She calls out three names, parties of four, six, twelve. Friends out for a good time. A sign by the entrance reads FILLMORE'S: WHERE YOUR FAMILY IS TREATED LIKE THE FIRST FAMILY!

I go back outside to wait for Beth and to breathe, slowly.

I text Beth to tell her I'm outside. When the phone vibrates a moment later I assume she's going to cancel. Why not?

Be there in two minutes. Hooray!

I hum songs to myself and stand near one of the young parking-lot trees. I touch the trunk and hum and breathe and wait.

Beth shows up looking adorable. And when I say this I want it to be clear that I value adorableness in girls. I can acknowledge *hotness* in girls. I know what all the standards of *hotness* are. I know that legs and ass and blond hair and big tits and skirts and tight shirts and lipstick and all those things mean *hotness.* But I have to admit that only some of those things really matter to me.

I cannot pretend to be unaroused by *hotness.* I just don't want to spend time with *hotness.*

I want to spend time with *adorable.*

Beth has her short hair pulled back with a green headband thing. She's wearing a spring-y skirt and lipstick. Her ears, her lips, her nose, all seem perfectly balanced on her face. Her forehead makes a smooth arc at her hairline. She is *adorable.*

Do I look at her breasts? Of course! Plus, I can tell I will definitely see down her shirt later and it won't even be on purpose. It will be a result of the natural movements of a dinner between people, as well as the semiautomatic glances of my eyes and the intentionally loose design of her shirt.

She picked the shirt. I'll do my best but cannot promise anything.

What am I supposed to do? Pretend like she's not a girl? Pretend like I haven't imagined what she looks like without clothes? Pretend I don't want to know, desperately, if she has big nipples or small? If she shaves? If she wears thongs? Or if she's more fantastic than any of those individual little sexy facts that would thrill me in the moment of discovery?

Will her laughter lose the power to make my heart hurt? Will we ever run out of things to talk about, serious or not? Will we hold hands tonight? Will I be close enough to inhale the soft smell of the shampoo or perfume that she chose for tonight? Will I be funny enough to make her laugh and make us both forget about time and place and circumstances beyond our control?

Will I be able to hold off a new round of anxiety and depression?

We hug. People look at us or they don't. I tune everything out, even the people close to our age, the jealous boys I see and the girls I'd normally let my eyes wander over just to take in a passing smile.

Our buzzer goes off and we sit and I think that maybe Jorie will appear after all. That maybe the hostess thought I said someone else's name. But no, the waiter is a dude with mutton chops and earrings and he's very happy we chose Fillmore's tonight. We send him off with drink orders.

"How are you feeling tonight?" Beth asks.

"I'm not sure how to respond!" I laugh.

"Why not?"

It's hard to explain why without sounding foolish.

"It's just been a weird couple of days." I unpeel the napkin wrap from the silverware.

"You were very down on the phone last night. Had me worried."

"I got better."

"But you still had a weird day today?"

"Yeah, I guess. We don't need to get into it, but my sister apparently doesn't work here anymore."

"Does that mean we're going to get crappy service?" Beth smiles and I smile and we talk about other things.

Here is a poem I write in my head:

This is the hour I hide everything
Behind my eyes
To see if you can see
All the trouble my brain's been brewing.

Yes, I feel I am the worst and you are the best
And yet, and yet,
Nothing bad unfolds as we sit,

Young and nervous,

Alive and bursting,

With futures that may not entwine.

Who am I?

Who am I to sabotage what may be too small

For even chaos to notice

And disassemble?

When Beth leaves to use the restroom I pull out my cell phone to check the time. It's flying by.

I have three texts from Derek, all of them begging me to let him know if I see Sally making out with some dude in the parking lot.

Slightly annoyed by this reminder of other people's concerns, I still manage to peek around to see if Derek's double agent girlfriend appears.

I notice her floating around the bar, over to the hostess station, stopping at tables. Normal shift manager responsibilities.

I text back that she's working and doesn't seem to be paying close attention to any heinous-looking dudes.

Me: She hasn't even been to the parking lot, from what I see.

Derek: Check her knees. Are there little pieces of gravel in her knees?

Me: What??

Derek: BJ in the parking lot. Ha!

Me: You are sad.

Derek: Good news, then. But keep an eye on her.

Me: I'm on a date, man. Give me a break.

Derek: It's not a date unless she touches you where you pee.

Me: Good night, loser.

I put the phone away as Beth returns.

"You got a hot date?" she says, noting the phone I'm slipping in my pocket.

"I do, actually." I smile at her.

She grins and her eyes break contact with mine. This feels like an important gesture.

"So I want to say that I'm glad you're feeling better and I'm glad we got to hang out tonight."

She twirls her straw and little bits of soda fleck the tabletop. She wipes them away with her palm.

"We should do this again," I say, because that's what people say when dates go well.

"I told my boyfriend I was coming here with you tonight."

Uggggggh. You know all those butterflies that live and party-till-they-puke in my stomach? Even they feel bad for me right now.

"What did *Drama Mavens* have to say?"

"I just told him the truth. That a good friend of mine needed cheering up!"

Now it's time for me to break off eye contact. It's time for me to break off everything. I poke ice with my straw. I pick up the little ball of straw paper and unroll it, then twist it into a thin, toothpick-y shape. I twirl it between my finger and thumb. I pay very close attention to this and try not to listen.

"Are you okay, James?"

"Yeah. It's fine. I just thought. I just got myself into a place where my hopes . . ." I look out the windows, but it's dark outside and the windows are tinted and I can see more of my reflection than anything else. Seeing myself is not what I need right now.

"You just sounded so terrible on the phone last night," she says.

"I shouldn't have called. I should have called someone else."

Beth's face defies interpretation. Mostly because my eyes hurt and my brain races and my breathing has become cold and slow.

"It's okay that you called. I just shouldn't have pretended like this was a date. I have a boyfriend."

"A guy that you don't really like. Or that doesn't like you." I'm trying to be mean, but I'm also sure of all the things she's said about him. What was the point of all those little secrets being divulged to me? She confided in me but now wants to pretend like I don't know any of that information? She dresses for a date but we're not on a date?

"It's complicated." She looks around, as if we're making a scene. But no one's paying attention to us. Even I don't want to know who we are.

"It's not that I don't like you, James. If things were different this would be a different kind of night."

"We should get the check," I suggest, because I can't listen to someone else tell me how my life could be different if it were different.

It is the longest ten minutes of my life so far.

Outside she hugs me. She doesn't press herself close to me. She doesn't press her hands very hard on my back. She doesn't let the hug linger, draw out, define itself. I imagine she's looking off at some stranger and wants to shrug. My eyes are closed because that seems like the right thing to do for a hug like this.

I sit on one of the benches after she's gone. I guess all the poems I've composed will get buried in my closet. I guess the website literary magazine will get scrapped. Roy will be pissed that we got him jazzed for an idea that we're scrapping for non-poetry-related reasons.

What would Whitman think about all this? He didn't write about girls, but he had to have loved someone. His hurt heart had to feel the same, right?

I want to pull out a copy of *Leaves of Grass* right now, but the paperback version that always accompanies me sits at home on my dresser. Why bring Whitman on a date with a girl who doesn't like him? She would not be impressed. And here I am in desperate need of him.

I fidget. I pace around. I consider walking home or to Jorie's (if I can remember the way). I can't call my dad for a ride home. He'll know that things didn't go well even if I lie about it. Because I won't be able to lie about it. I'll just mumble my answers and tell him nothing bad happened. Sometimes he does know things that he should not comment on. Sometimes I just need to be left alone. And sometimes the people I want to bother me let me down.

I see Sally come outside and light up a cigarette. She's alone. I watch her. I want to know if she's a villain too. She's standing there very sure of herself. She looks like everyone else in Fillmore's except she has a phone clipped to her belt. Must be great to have authority, even a small amount of it. She can feel like she has some purpose in the world.

Then I get more mad and wonder *Why Derek?* Why did she pick him over anyone? A girl like that? He can't go to bars or clubs with her. She can't expect him to buy her things. He's not a romantic guy. He's just a guy. He's my friend, but there has to be something wrong with her to need a relationship with a high school kid.

Sally's texting and smoking, smiling, thrilling at her little life.

With a stomach full of irritated butterflies, I begin walking over to her and then follow as she walks inside.

In the main waiting area I tap her on the shoulder. She turns around with a pretend smile, the kind that's always ready for a drunk and dissatisfied burger-stuffed customer.

"Sally."

She doesn't recognize me. Why would she?

"It's James. Derek's friend."

"Oh, right, right! I didn't recognize you with two good arms. How are you?"

"I'm good. But I'd be better if you told me why you're screwing around on Derek?"

"Excuse me?"

"He got a text message he wasn't supposed to." I watch as her face gets pale. I think. It's hard to tell in the Fillmore's lighting.

"Seems like you are waiting to see The Hype tonight?"

But now her potentially pale face changes to a healthy-colored smirk.

"He sent you to complain about a text message?"

"It seemed strange that you would be excited to do something on a Friday night with someone other than your fiancé and your underage boyfriend!"

I say this loud because fuck Sally and fuck Beth and fuck my parents and fuck me, most of all.

Sally starts walking away and I yell things at her that I should be ashamed of, but shame has no place in my mind right now. I'm racing along, buzzing with the manic energy I yearn to harness but never can.

"You think he doesn't brag about all the dirty things you do in the parking lot of Fillmore's?!"

Yes, I say that out loud. Very out loud.

Families go from enjoying their Millard Shakes to whispering about the crazy boy yelling at the manager. Couples on dates complain about the terrible atmosphere. Food service people apologize and distract with talk of appetizers and desserts.

I know how all these people operate. I know that they're all just going to pretend like I'm not here trying to tear the walls down with my *fucking barbaric yaawwwwwwppppp!*

Did I say some of that out loud? I'm very scared that I don't know.

A few tall, sideburns-sporting waiters and bus boys come over and urge me to leave.

"The great procreant urge of the world is not an excuse for sluttiness!" I turn and run and run some more.

Whitman would not be proud of this behavior.

At least he's dead and never met me.

31.

I KEEP RUNNING. I'm not a runner, though, and I'm dressed for a date, so I get tired and hot quickly. I try to think of the direction of Jorie's house, but I'm confused and too upset to recall the map in my mind.

What the hell do I do now?

I call Derek.

"What the fuck did you do to me this time?" he screams. "Sally just called me screaming about my asshole friend calling her a *whore* in front of the entire restaurant?!"

"I'm sorry. I got mad. I got really mad because Beth got weird and then I saw Sally and thought she was cheating on you with The Hype."

I hear Derek talking to Flip in the pizza shop. Something about handwriting, bad addresses. Normal concerns.

"Why did you even say anything to her? I just said *watch* her. "

"You're my friend. I needed to defend you!"

"Flip, there is no street with that name. Jesus Christ, man, learn how to write! Or listen!"

I hear Flip screaming at Derek and maybe Derek screaming back, but I'm standing in a quiet strip mall parking lot, so everything seems loud and blurred together in my phone's earpiece.

"I'm sorry, Derek."

"Stop talking."

"I didn't do it to ruin your life."

"Stop talking!"

I can't figure out who he's addressing, so I shut up to be safe.

I'm quiet and listening to pizza shop shouting and then there's three beeps and the call is dead.

Calling back to ask for a ride seems out of the question.

Wandering seems reasonable. Whitman wandered through nature, stopped to loaf, stopped to ponder.

> *This, then, is life;*
> *Here is what has come to the surface after so many*
> *throes and convulsions.*

Whitman didn't write this for moping moments. It's at a moment when he celebrates the cosmos. But I am incapable of celebration right now. I am a rotting oak, aware of the creaking of my diseased trunk. Gravity strengthens its constant pull. My limbs weaken. I will tumble, though I cannot tumble. My responsibilities crack and groan because I have been irresponsible.

I walk west, or what I think is west, because that's what Whitman might suggest in a dark time.

Why can't I recall the times that Whitman speaks of darkness? Why can't I feel connected to him, even, at this low moment?

I recognize a street, a landmark eyesore, a streetlight, a bend in the road. Wandering has brought me to the bug-filled garage apartment of Jorie. Something has gone right. I plod up the steps, which creak like my soul. Was the soul designed to bend like a tree? Maybe. Does it have joints that squeak? Maybe.

Knocking on the door produces no results. A light glows in the window, but it's a dim one. Either she can't afford higher-wattage bulbs or she left a light on for her late night return home.

Dr. Bird pecks on my brain. I try to swish her away with my hand.

"Do you need drugs?" she asks.

"I don't want to be a zombie."

"Do zombies get depressed?"

"I'm afraid it will mean I feel nothing. I'll have numb eyes. I'll lose the ability to take pictures or write poems."

"Are you sure of any of these possibilities?"

I say I'm not sure of anything, but I'm afraid of losing what little connection to my real brain that I have left.

"What if your real mind is already gone behind a curtain? What if the drugs will move the curtain?"

"I don't think drugs move curtains."

"Could they move mountains? Huge mountains of anxiety that are in the way of your real self?"

"I'm not sure."

"Are you sure that your real self is this anxiety-ridden, bursting, twisting, unhappy, buzzing, hate-filled, meandering, overtired sleepless boy?"

I say I'm not sure who I am.

"Then would drugs really make a difference? Would the drugs be any worse?"

"I don't want to be artificial."

"You want to be nonfunctional?"

"I would rather malfunction than sit and stare at a wall like an unplugged coffeepot."

"Is this choice a result of anxiety and depression?"

I do not respond. I will ignore Dr. Bird until Jorie comes home or I fall asleep.

Dr. Bird says: "Don't you wish you would wake up one day and celebrate yourself? Don't you wish you would wake up one day and celebrate yourself? Don't you wish you would wake up one day and celebrate yourself?"

I want to scream at my brain, but I'm afraid of waking up Jorie's landlord and then getting her kicked out. It seems like I've already ruined enough lives tonight.

32.

JORIE WAKES ME UP around one a.m. She's alone, standing near the top step. There's not enough room for her to get up on the landing and kick me or poke my eye.

"What are you doing here?" She has a smoke-strained voice.

"I came to see you. You weren't home."

"I know I wasn't."

My back hurts from being bent weird in my sleep. I move to get out of the way of her door.

"I went to Fillmore's tonight. They said you didn't work there anymore."

Jorie unlocks her door. We go inside. She doesn't say anything about her job; I don't want to ask her where she's been tonight because I'm not her mother or father. I can't think of anything casual to say.

"I'm really tired, James. I'd like to hang out, but . . ."

"I don't have a ride home."

"I don't have a car."

"I know. I just. I can't call Dad to get me now."

She says I can crash on the floor. She pours a huge glass of water and explains she's trying to avoid a hangover.

"Did they fire you?"

"Sort of. I think I technically quit." She chugs the water. "They get to fill out the paperwork, so they'll find a way to screw me out of unemployment."

"I've been trying to get Mom and Dad to agree to let you come home," I admit as a way to cheer her up.

"You don't have to do that."

"Well, if you need to, I might have it figured out soon."

"I'm sure they won't let me."

"If I get you back into school, he will."

"That school will not take me back."

As Jorie makes herself a peanut butter sandwich, she licks peanut butter off the knife. This makes her seem very hungry.

"It doesn't matter. I got out of that school a little earlier than everyone else. That's it."

"What happened with Gina?"

My sister rubs her forearm. I take a glance to see if she's

been cutting herself, but the light in the room refuses to illuminate anything.

Jorie starts recounting the day of the fight, but nothing sounds important—woke up on time, Dad irritated her as usual, she forgot homework, she passed a pop quiz. Then, when she finally starts describing the fight with Gina, it sounds like an event in a small foreign country that she heard about on a scratchy AM radio. It's not something that happened to her, just something that happened. I ask little questions, mostly trying to steer her to explain what set the whole thing off, but she's stuck in the violence of it, how she lost control of herself, how she really wanted to hurt someone badly that week. By the time she gets to the moment things exploded, she only remembers that she wasn't wearing socks and that Mom had thrown out one of her favorite T-shirts and an angry roaring drowned out the sound of the hallway.

"But what did Gina *do* to set you off?"

"When I saw her, she was smiling. She looked so damn happy, like nothing could ever hurt her. Ever."

Jorie sits on the floor with her sandwich.

"Did you ever get so mad," she asks, tears pouring easily from her eyes, "that the whole world became flat and all you could see was anger-orange?"

I say nothing. It's too late to admit that I've never felt such an intense anger. Even earlier tonight, when I made a spectacle in the restaurant, I didn't feel like I was there as I yelled at Sally and customers and busboys. My real self was outside, waiting for my foolish body to start running.

I want to press her for the truth, a real, concrete fact about what happened, but we're both drained.

"You can sleep on the floor," she says. "I'll get you a blanket."

I text the Brute that I'm staying over at Jorie's. I hope that will be enough to keep him from killing me.

33.

I KNOW I'VE PISSED my father off good, because he hits me.

It's the first time my father's hit me in a long, long time. Years. Even back when I was little I only got hit for breaking things in the house or losing money. My mom used to smack at me when I was hyper or if I talked back, but I was good at avoiding her. Jorie was always more willing to take a hit; she told me once that Dad would get more aggressive if he missed, so it was better to let him land a couple right away so he'd be satisfied. I remember that she had a huge red mark on her back when she told me this. It was a weird moment, because Jorie was old enough to be shy about her body but she showed me this welt and was trying to brag about her ability to take a hit.

I could never adopt this strategy, but he also never seemed to maintain his focus when he missed. It's like he never had his heart into hitting me. And then I realized neither of them had hit me in months, then years.

So, when he hits me mid-tirade, it surprises us both. A whack to the temple so forceful and just out of the blue that I spin around and get hit a second time, less hard, possibly as punishment for being cartoonish.

In the moment I think something stupid: *This* is a reason to be depressed.

I am grounded for the foreseeable future. My father yells at me with the kind of ire people usually reserve for an outburst a few days before writing a manifesto and then shooting office coworkers. I can't even follow his argument for why I'm a terrible son.

Let's just all understand, though, that I agree.

In my room I stare up at the tree and simmer in a self-loathing that makes me hate the photos and the stupid effort I went through to tape it all together and affix it to the ceiling. I could have done something more productive.

Of course it would be okay to be depressed if I got abused as much as Jorie. But I'm not. So then there's something wrong with my wiring. I'm predisposed or programmed to be depressed. How horrible is that? Jorie was a mess last night and she's not even in the house suffering under my parents' regime.

I know my parents aren't swinging by her apartment for coffee, cake, and a quick smack. She and I seem to be poisoned with sadness in our blood.

Maybe this is why Jorie started cutting herself. To see if there was something different in her blood.

I'm not confined to my room, but I don't leave it. My mother brings me a sandwich for dinner; I leave the plate untouched on the bathroom sink.

By ten-thirty on Saturday night I'm at my worst moment. I check my phone and e-mail obsessively for signs of connection from Derek, Beth, or even any Facebook friends. I hit refresh again and again. Spam messages give me false joy; I infuriate myself.

Attempts to capture anxieties in my journal fail, despite all the free time.

Around two in the morning, I write a poem. It's the only thing that happens.

The oak grows out from the inside

old.

Rot licks slow.

The tree is upset.

Rooting in wrong places,

meeting up with concrete, buckling the ground

for kids on bikes to jump or tumble over.

The bugs crawl up, crawl in,

limbs get limp,

sway with less affection,

exaggerated in the dusk's storms.

The leaves flash white,

a mirror of clouds,

and no one knows it's too late

until a branch lets go,

hanging by dried-out muscle.

34.

I HAVEN'T EATEN SINCE the dinner with Beth. It's Sunday but I'm not hungry. I spend most of the day in my boxers, under my covers, sleeping. I tell my mom I'm sick, so she brings me soup and a peanut butter sandwich for every meal. It's gray outside, which doesn't help. My mood has grown cold. My eyes feel puffy. I'm congested. Maybe it's emotions, maybe it's phlegm.

For the first time in weeks, I return to that practical question: Why don't I just kill myself?

When I think about offing myself, I take a cue from Homer and begin *in medias res.* I think about being in the moment of doing it or having just done it. I think about myself as a crime scene or hovering over the moment of last hopes. I take pleasure in the fantasy of someone finding me, of amping up their guilt and sorrow as much as possible.

Then, after I've held my breath underwater as long as possible, so to speak, I jump back to the procuring of devices: How would I get a gun? Where would I tie the noose? Would a whole bottle of ibuprofen actually kill me?

Most of all, I want to cease. Goodbye, worries, end-of-semester projects, attendance, staying awake, gym class. My stupid haircuts, gone. No need to worry about colleges, girls, or disintegrating friendships.

Pleasure exists in these thoughts. In the throes of suicidal thoughts, the counting down of reasons both delays the act and encourages it. This must be what drug addicts love: teetering.

I am not a kind person. I have been a bad brother. A bad friend. I hate my parents. My parents hate me. I do not try in school. Girls do not like me. I am not interesting. I read books people do not care for. I watch movies to enjoy cinematography and not explosions. I do not drink enough alcohol. I do not enjoy parties. I cannot relax enough to relax. I will never be able to extinguish my worries.

Then Whitman wakes up and, despite what I expect, he helps me stay focused on death.

Has any one supposed it lucky to be born?
I hasten to inform him or her it is just as lucky to
die.

That's a good one. True. Worthy of a yawp, if I had the energy.

Oh, but then there's this:

> *Was it doubted that those who corrupt their own*
> *bodies conceal themselves?*
> *And if those who defile the living are as bad as they*
> *who defile the dead?*

So, really, he can't refrain from judging suicides. But fuck you, Whitman, because my sister defiled her body with little cuts while trying to find the joy that you so easily see in spears of grass. How come that couldn't save her? How come trees can't save me? How come we didn't see bright joy in the world, or in ourselves?

Later, as my father drives me to the pizzeria, his gassy, grumpy body reeking of judgment and anger and disappointment, I can't help but wonder how little he knows about the depth of my sadness. The depth of my very being. Will he be upset to find me dead, or relieved? Maybe he'll use me as an excuse. Maybe I'll help him seal a few real estate deals.

"I'm sorry, Dilbert, but I've just been so distracted with the death of my son that I haven't been able to come up with a decent counterbid."

"Gee, Dale, that's all right. We'll accept whatever offer you've got."

Cue fake tears. Cue manly back-patting. Cue check writing.

At the pizza shop, nothing happens. It's a Sunday night. A few orders come in. No one picks them up, it seems, but the pizzas disappear. I assume I'm ringing people up. Some other dude is working delivery, but he spends the night texting while sitting in the booth by the door. I forget his name. Usually Derek and I work together, but I bet he switched nights to stay away from me.

A pizzeria seems like the dumbest place to be depressed. Maybe I'm in hell.

I wipe down the already wiped-down tables and chairs. I think about what I would miss if I died.

Sometimes I urge my body to develop an illness that will kill me. So that I will know something is wrong inside and I can withhold the hurt and decay until it's too late.

And they would say, "Why didn't you tell us something was wrong?"

And I would say, "You didn't notice. You never noticed. Something was wrong the whole time."

That, I think, would be the most satisfying thing. Has anyone ever committed suicide with a self-willed cancer?

I have not eaten since Friday, I remember. It might be causing the headache that squints my eyes. The smell of pizza normally would exacerbate the situation, but I feel nothing in my stomach. A full, round nothing.

I check my phone for e-mails, texts, signs of life that I can grumble about.

There's a message from Jorie:

> J - Sorry about the other night. Haven't been doing great. I think you know what I mean. But there's nothing wrong with being down sometimes. We should hang out and listen to some music. I borrowed a hard drive from my friend Dutch. It's got lots of crazy stuff that I think we'll both love. I miss your tree pics!
>
> Stay chipper, skipper!
>
> Love, Jorie

Flip finds me crying over by the pizza prep counter. I expect him to freak out—what's a guy supposed to do when he finds some stupid kid tearing up over the floured prep station?

I'm not sure how long he's been standing there, but he doesn't leave me alone. I start wiping my eyes and apologizing.

"It's all right, guy, it's all right," he says. "What do you need? You want to go out back for a minute?"

I nod, thinking he'll leave me alone, but he follows me outside. I'm not sure I can handle wisdom from Flip right now. But he just stands with me. He doesn't look at me, he looks out at the broken-down fence that's supposed to keep people from the back lot, apparently.

"I don't know what happened." I sniff, wipe my eyes, and try to compose myself.

"It happens," he says.

I want to explain myself, but I hold off. Flip doesn't know me. I'm already talking to Dr. Bird and to a therapist—no need to involve more strangers.

"I saw a movie once where someone was making food and they cried in it," Flip says. "And then when people ate the food they all became so sad that they all started crying."

I say I've never seen that movie.

"I don't remember what it was called. A woman I dated made me watch it. I told her I didn't like it, but that part made me really think. You know?"

I nod. I'm afraid to think about what kind of emotions I could be getting from food.

"It's okay to cry. Men have to cry sometimes. You take a minute." Flip goes inside.

I feel better but also worse.

All these thoughts of suicide suddenly seem childish. I can't even imagine myself taking the steps to do anything. How did I come full circle so quickly? It's like I shook off an entire weekend funk with one set of public tears.

Jorie, Jorie. The only thing that I keep hanging on to. She doesn't need me to be strong for her. But she'll be mad if I kill myself. It would be worse than abandonment. It would be judgment and rejection. It would be the thing she might want to do but cannot. I'd get to it first. Then what would she do? Cut herself more? Less? Would she get a gun or some pills? She'd just be sad and mad and alone.

Maybe I should get on some drugs. It doesn't seem like the world or my brain will ever adjust to one another. I'm permanently lopsided. Maybe the drugs will keep me from crying at work.

I have to work another five days to afford a visit to Dr. Dora, though. And she said it might take a few more visits to really know for sure if I need drugs. And then it will probably take more time to get the drugs. And more time for them to work. By then I might be dead.

How come more people don't kill themselves, if it's this hard to stay afloat?

35.

THE NEXT DAY IN SCHOOL I think about Jorie's stupid sign-off (*Stay chipper, skipper!*) and realize I still have a mission. I spend the first three periods of the day working up the courage to confront VP VanO or Kunkel. This time, it's personal. Let's do this. Rock 'n' roll. All those action-movie-confrontation-scene clichés roar in my head.

During fourth period, I head to the principals' suite, trying to work up the courage to ask Mrs. Berry if VP VanO woud see me for a meeting.

I walk up to the turret that Mrs. Berry barricades herself behind and ask for the vice principal.

"He's not in right now but should be back. Is it important?"

"I need to talk to him about my sister." I look off at the offices to see if Mrs. Berry's telling the truth. I can't tell from here.

"Your sister?"

"Jorie Whitman."

"You're Jorie's brother?"

"Yes."

"How is she?" Mrs. Berry whispers this, which draws my attention to her completely. "I worry about her."

"She's okay. I'm not sure—were you here when she got kicked out?"

"I'm always here," she chuckles, and shuffles some meaningless papers.

"Can you tell me what happened?"

"Well, she was kicked out the day she fought with that Gina—you know that, right?"

"Yes," I say. "And the vice principal told me about the laptop."

"What laptop?"

"Mrs. Yao's laptop," I say with some excitement. More facts might exist in Mrs. Berry's brain.

"Mrs. Yao's laptop? Is that what happened?"

"What do you mean?"

"Well, I handled the paperwork to get the laptop replaced. She said she dropped it. Did your sister hit Gina with it?" Mrs. Berry looks offended by the prospect.

"No!" I whisper strongly. "The vice principal says she threw it at Mrs. Yao, but Mrs. Yao says that's not what happened."

"I didn't know about that."

"This is why I'm here." I tell Mrs. Berry about the report VP VanO read to me and how Gina might know more than she's willing to admit.

"Well, Gina might be lying." Mrs. Berry looks around. I feel like a spy or a detective. Someone with a secret purpose.

"*Why*, though?"

"Gina was there in the library with your sister."

Someone should take my picture and put it in the dictionary entry for *exasperated*.

"Are you sure you don't want to talk to a counselor?" Mrs. Berry suddenly suggests. "Students seem to like Miss Tebler. She is better at the more social aspects of everything."

I feel her eyes dart over my shoulder. Not surprisingly, I see VanO and Principal Kunkel chatting over by one of the offices.

"Mrs. Berry," I whisper, "just tell me what happened with Jorie."

In a regular voice, Mrs. Berry says she's going to make an appointment for me with Miss Tebler for a few days from now. She hands me a slip of paper and tells me to make sure I show up on time.

Go, she mouths. As I walk past VanO, I suppress the urge to grab him and shake answers out of him. He's frail enough to break apart in my angry hands. But Mrs. Berry must know the danger, because she calls out to the heads of the school that they have messages waiting.

Out in the hallway I look at the note and see that Mrs. Berry has written:

Tebler's on vacation until Monday.

Come @ 9:30a.m.

She knows.

36.

AFTER SCHOOL I RUN up to my room. I don't need to be home to call Dr. Dora, but I feel the most comfortable when buffeted by my room's four walls. I plan to whisper in case my mother decides to listen outside my door while pretending to put away some towels.

As I listen to the phone ring all I can do is hope to get her voice mail. I don't think I can admit out loud, in my house, where the walls have ears and the door has eyes, that I want to hurt myself.

I get Dr. Dora's voice mail. The universe favors me.

"Dr. Dora, this is James Whitman. Your new patient. Who you met last week. I was calling to see if I could get in to see you next week and if there's a way I can pay later. I'm having trouble with money. I hope you understand."

I end the call and immediately whisper: "I want to die. I want to die."

I distract myself from this thought by calculating how much money I have, how much I can get, how much I need. I start thinking about things I can sell—books, DVDs, CDs, clothes. I bag up some things and feel like I have too much crap anyway. I should sell it all or just give it away. I should minimize. I should not have things for myself other than the necessary amount of clothes, a pair of shoes, a toothbrush. Everything is expendable.

At work, I ask Flip if I can make more money somehow.

"Well, I don't need any drivers," he says. "I got Derek and my dummy nephew. You can't even drive."

"Can I make pizzas?"

"No, guy, you don't have the hands." He holds up his hands as if to prove the point.

"Have you even ever looked at my hands?" I hold up mine in response.

"I don't need to look. I know! You need the hands of a man to make pizza after pizza."

I want to tell him that I'm more than capable of spreading ketchup on cardboard. I want to tell him that my hands can put up with all the burns and grease and flour. But he's shaking his head.

"I hired you because you are Derek's friend. He said you needed a job, I gave you a job. I have three nieces that will need a job soon too. They won't ask for more money. They won't ask to make pizzas."

"Are you firing me?"

"Not yet."

This is the same guy who didn't mock me for crying. Now he's a grinning bastard.

The night mopes on. I ring a few people up. We get a bunch of big orders. A Little League coach comes in and pays with a hundred-dollar bill. It sits below the cash tray in the drawer for an hour, taunting me. That's therapy. And medication. That's my life—literally. I can pay for sanity. Or, at least, I can pay for a break from insanity.

How long would it take Flip to notice missing money? He can't even write down orders the right way. I've seen him labor over the register at night.

Perhaps if I littered some bills on the floor, over near the trash or something. If he went crazy looking for the missing money and saw some on the floor he'd think the money got dropped, maybe thrown out. It might work.

Maybe I shouldn't steal an exact amount. Maybe I should steal a hundred and seven dollars and forty-three cents, or something, so that they don't think it's just big bills missing.

Maybe I should just knock over the tip jar toward the end of the night too, confuse things more.

Maybe I could just bash Flip over the head with one of the metal pans he uses to store pepperoni.

When did I become so despicable?

As the night progresses I pocket fives and tens, but then I get greedy and take the hundred. When I get home I've got enough money for therapy and enough anxiety and guilt to keep me up for three years.

37.

DR. DORA ASKS ME how I've been. I say there's no easy way to answer that.

"Anxious?"

"Yes."

"Depressed?"

"Oh, yes."

She asks me to tell her how I felt this weekend, but when I begin to tell her *why* I got depressed, she stops me.

"No, James. You have to listen carefully—I want to know *how it felt.* Not *why you felt it.*"

I'm a little perturbed by this splitting of hairs.

"I think it's important that you know why, though," I urge.

"I will ask you the *why* later. First, let's go through the *how.*"

I sigh and look off to the right. There's a crappy picture of a gray-toned sailboat in a bright silver frame. It's got seagulls. I freaking hate seagulls.

"It felt. Depressing."

"Do better than that."

"I don't know. I didn't leave my room."

"Good. What else? Did you do anything in your room?"

"I slept. I stayed in bed. Didn't eat. Didn't shower."

"Did you check e-mail, Facebook, cell phone?" She's poised to write down my answer.

"I think so. But not as often as normal. My phone was off, actually."

She nods and writes. I answer a few more questions and feel even stupider for having been depressed.

"Did you think about suicide?"

I hesitate.

"James?"

"Yes."

My eyes water. It's too much, all this turning inside out. I feel like I'm always turned inside out. That my nerves have become extra sensitive because of all this exposure to the world.

"What stopped you?" she asks.

"Nothing."

"Are you going to go home and kill yourself, then?"

"No!"

"Something stopped you."

"I got an e-mail from my sister."

She asks me why this, of all things, stopped me.

"Because. I don't know. Because she seemed to know I needed a message at that moment. And I know she probably had to borrow someone's laptop just to send it. And that probably was the only reason she borrowed the laptop. So I had a moment where I felt like someone was thinking about me."

Dr. Dora appears as if she's about to ask me something, but my brain has to explain.

"I'm really guilty. All the time. I feel really guilty about Jorie."

"Why are you guilty?"

"Because I didn't help her! I didn't stand up for her, ever. When my parents said things about her, I just agreed that she caused trouble or didn't try at school. I agreed! And then the night she got thrown out I didn't come to her rescue. I didn't stand up with her or run outside to help her up! I didn't call my dad an asshole for being such a goddamn . . . tyrant! I didn't! I didn't do anything."

I'm crying, but I can speak. I keep speaking. I keep trying to talk through the guilt, to pull it out of me and toss it into the air where it will die like a virus, but the barbs and hooks of guilt hold strong in my lungs. My lungs hitch as I cry.

“She got in trouble for things that I did and I didn’t own up to them. And she never even thought it was me. I used my parents’ credit card to buy stuff online and they said it was her, that she was buying stuff for her and her friends. She never even asked if it was me. They yelled at her for two hours and hit her—they didn’t even think it was me. They didn’t think I was capable of screwing up.”

I think about the money I stole just to have the benefit of this confession and I cry more. I feel like I’ve been crying forever, but I can’t stop it. I have to keep going until someone tells me something that will make this all work out.

38.

MENTALLY, I HAVEN'T BEEN in school. I've been attending, but the assignments cover topics that merge with things that aren't really part of school. In history we're learning about the assassination of Archduke Franz Ferdinand, who wrote some songs about dancing and sex. In physics we're learning about time travel, perpetually. In English we're reading *The House of Seven Samurai.* In gym, it's all the same, of course. My gym clothes smell like they haven't been washed since November. Have I been to school this year? Ever? Has someone else been acting as me?

Derek sits with me at lunch even though his friends from his grade all clearly think he's a dork for doing so. It's been five days since we last spoke.

"I told Sally that we had to break up."

"*You* broke up with *her?*" I asked.

"It's too much. I can't keep lying to my mom."

"I'm impressed that you can turn down all that sex, considering your terrible reputation on the Internet."

I'm trying to make light of the situation. Again.

"Did you steal money from the pizza shop?" he asks.

"Huh?"

"The register was off by a bunch on Sunday night. Flip's been crazy all week trying to figure out what happened."

"Oh."

"I told him it was his nephew. But Flip says you were all sorts of weird on Sunday."

"Huh." I have reverted to monosyllabic communication with the hopes that I will be found incapable of going to trial. ("He's a caveman, your honor! He can't testify or be tried by a jury of his peers. Unless you can find more cavemen, that is." Laughter, freedom, etc.)

"I want to know what kind of 'weird,' but you and I have larger issues to discuss."

"I broke down crying." This comes out surprisingly easy. It's as if confessing to Dr. Dora loosened up my tongue.

"Crying?" Derek hasn't looked me in the eye since sitting down with his lunch. But suddenly he's looking at me. I have never given him credit for being a thoughtful guy. Now I realize that he's always been thoughtful. He got me out of my house by getting me a job.

"Do you know what my house is like, Derek?"

"A little," he says. "You tell me stuff without telling me stuff."

"I did steal the money."

Derek pounds his fist against the white table and curses, loud. People at the surrounding tables look at him.

"I'm sorry, man, I just—my parents wouldn't pay for me to go see a therapist. I've been seeing one secretly and I have to pay her when I go."

"Why didn't you just tell me you needed money? I could have lent you some. Why did you have to steal from the job I got you?"

"Flip said he was going to get rid of me once his nieces are old enough to run the register. It pissed me off!"

"He doesn't have nieces, man! It's a joke! He says that to everyone—haven't you noticed that?" Derek is amused and pissed. I envy his ability to mix those emotions.

I say that I didn't notice. I don't pay attention to those things.

"Man, you need to return that money. I'll give you money for therapy. Even though you've fucked me on multiple fronts lately."

An apology starts to form, but then Dr. Dora rears her stern head in my mind. I tell her head that an apology here is appropriate. She doesn't speak. Am I supposed to do something other than apologize? She doesn't speak.

Why am I having an awkward exchange with an imaginary version of my real therapist? Where is Dr. Bird for stuff like this? Suddenly Dr. Bird appears. It's the back of her; she wobbles away from me, then circles. When I see her little black eye, she stops, cocks her head. She wants to ask me something but doesn't. I want to ask her what's happening, but then I recognize that a silence has been stretching itself out like bubblegum in the real world where birds don't talk and my therapist is more than just a head and Derek sits there waiting for me to say I'm sorry.

"I've been having a hard time." I scratch my cheek, my nose, above my eye. I'm trying to hide behind something. "I've been really depressed. I am depressed. Really bad. I think about killing myself."

Derek shifts in his cafeteria chair.

"I haven't tried, but I have thought about it. For months and months. I wake up and fall asleep with the same thoughts. Then I stopped thinking about it. But after this weekend, I've been thinking about it again."

"Shit."

There are lists of things on the Internet about what you shouldn't say to someone who admits to depression and suicidal thoughts. "Shit" is probably the wrong thing to say. However, it seems right. If it's the *only* thing Derek says I will probably lose faith in him as a friend.

"What do you need me to do?" he asks. "I mean that—I don't want to pretend that I know what it's like. But this sounds like *for real* depression. Like one step from one of those slow-motion commercials with blue-tinted shots of people who sleep all the time."

"It's hard to describe." I look around the cafeteria. I wonder how many people in the room would say that I should just *think happy thoughts* or *get organized* or *decide on a college and career.* I wonder how many of them cut themselves. I see girls laughing with guys. I see guys moody and alone. I see girls checking their faces in small mirrors. I see girls not eating. I see guys waving around iced teas as they tell dynamic jokes. I see teachers mope through the room. I see the cashier and the food service ladies smile for some kids, frown at others. I see smirks, behind-the-back points and laughs. I see all these things and I wonder what these people see in me? In Derek?

"Derek, what can I do to un-fuck your world up?"

"Don't worry about it," he laughs. "I'm not sure I can be un-fucked at this point. And you've got your own shit to deal with."

I say that I'll give the money back to Flip and apologize and quit. I'll make sure Flip knows that Derek didn't have anything to do with it. Or his nephew.

"You can't quit if you need therapy money."

"I'll get my parents to pay somehow."

He tries to object and brainstorm ways for me to keep my job, but I insist that *my* plan will need to be *the* plan. Not because it's the best idea, but because I'll feel guilty otherwise.

In my mind Dr. Bird says, "Good good good good."

39.

I SOUND MY MORNING YAWP! I blast out my inner glow at the sunshine to try and shout it down. To have it lift me up. For someone, somewhere, to see me!

> *Dazzling and tremendous how quick the sun-rise*
> *would kill me,*
> *If I could not now and always send sun-rise out of*
> *me!*

I care not what clothes I wear today. I care not about my hair. I linger on the smells I've accumulated overnight in my warm bed. I consider letting the beautiful fragrance of my living, breathing self speak for me, but then I shower and shave and brush my teeth, remembering that the world has moved past the nineteenth century and into a world of germs and deodorant.

Still, though, I feel an energy in my body electric. I feel the blood in my veins; the marrow in my bones pulses and my very bones glow.

Did someone slip me drugs in my dreams? Mayhaps!

I ignore my mother and father, saying nothing, not even a yawp. I find it best to keep my mouth closed and my mind racing to get out of the house without worries. My father does not consider me for more than a moment—I am the strange thing that came from him. My mother seems perturbed by my silent hand gestures, shrugs, smiles, waves, but I'm out the door before she can complain, before I can crumble and be the sullen boy that absorbs little comments about how I should compose myself and how my clothes are wrinkled and how I have four hundred stupid chores waiting for me when I return from hours of school.

I burst out my front door and greet trees in my mind, zagging to touch trees that rarely feel my palm on them. I am in a rush but without true direction. I jump into a backyard to touch a crabapple tree because I've never touched one of them before. A dog comes barking after me, a little yap-yap that I barely escape. It jumps and throws itself in a tight 360 spin with each little bark. I laugh and laugh!

At the park across from school I hug trees, pressing my cheek against the trunks, wrapping my arms as far around them as possible. My fingertips twitch to reach each other.

I look at the red marks on my inner arms and decide this does not count as defiling. I even absolve Jorie because she did not intend to ruin her body; she sought peace through pain. I do not condone the method, but the method didn't destroy her. It only helped her from being destroyed.

"Walt Whitman, I'm sorry for cursing you out. I don't think you would punish Jorie for cutting because you would see her suffering. You saw suffering and cared, you cared for the strangers, the soldiers, the women, the lonely. You cared and just wanted people to see the joy in themselves both in their souls and their bodies. You would do the same for Jorie, and maybe me.

"So, I apologize, Walt Whitman."

I walk on, feeling less manic but still bright. I'm not falling flat on the face of misery just yet. It might approach me quietly, but I'm not going to wave it in. I'm going to let it approach me face-to-face.

I weave my arm through a huge bush. The leaves tickle my arm hairs.

As I get to the sidewalk and prepare to cross, I see Beth walking. She's not checking her phone or distracted by friends. She's alone, walking slower than normal. She's not sad, yet she doesn't seem lively. She normally bounces when she walks. Today she looks like she wants to blend in with the plain walkers. The people who don't like poetry. Who don't want to look other people in the eye, or deep into the eyes of others.

Part of me still burns embarrassed for my assumptions. Part of me hopes that she dumped Martin. Part of me thinks back to how I broke my arm trying to impress her. That poor little Tastykake wrapper. That poor bus driver.

I look both ways and cross the street. I swoop up next to Beth and say hello with the kind of ease I never thought possible.

"Hey, James." She smiles and it's not the best smile she's ever given me, but it's real and not about happiness or love or anything abstract. *It's nice to see a friend in the morning,* it says.

We walk a bit and I have many urges—to apologize, to explain myself, to say we can start over . . . or at least jump backwards, prior to our Fillmore's dinner. But time travel isn't possible, and an explanation doesn't seem necessary and an apology seems dramatic.

Instead, I ask about her week and tell her about some

poems I'm working on and we make a plan to meet this afternoon to finish the website. It's like we've gotten past weirdness without even worrying about what the weirdness means.

I guess sometimes life can be easy if I let it.

40.

AFTER DINNER, I SPEND a while staring up at my photo tree. It seems dusty and the photos' corners are curling, ruining the illusion of connectivity between all the different limbs and trunks. I should get more tape, but I just stay on my back, afraid to disturb the relative peace I'm feeling.

Of course, my phone starts buzzing.

"Yo!" I say with both mock and genuine enthusiasm.

"*Get away from the window!*" Derek yells to someone on his end. "Dude. I need a favor."

He sounds very concerned but also like he wants to laugh.

"I need you to come over and help me get Sally away from my house."

He explains that Sally showed up on his front lawn ten minutes ago and started throwing clumps of dirt at his bedroom window.

Derek yells at his sisters and they yell back. Accusations, threats, dirt clumps knocking against the window. Laughter, too.

"Dude, if my mom comes home or the cops show up, I am screwed!"

"What the hell am I supposed to do?"

"Anything!"

I tell him I'll be over as soon as possible.

I grab my camera bag and hop on my bike, feeling like a weirdo journalist off to cover a big story.

I haven't biked to Derek's since last year, and I feel like I haven't really enjoyed riding my bike since eighth grade, when pedal-powered travel dominated my outdoor movements. Still, I remember sidewalk buckles and low curbs I can jump over with ease. All the old muscle memories return vividly, almost as if the smell of the moving air, the sound of the tires on asphalt, and my bending knees spark a part of my brain back to life.

This is happiness.

As I approach Derek's house, I see someone on his front lawn, peeking in windows, banging on the front door. If the cops don't show up in seconds, I'll be shocked. I start taking pictures. I'm not sure if I'll have the balls to do anything else, but I figure I can take a few pictures and see what happens.

I get a shot of Sally lofting one of Derek's mom's plants over the roof of the split-level. I get a shot of her screaming at the front door. I get a shot of her ripping grass out of the yard with both hands. Video would be more appropriate, but that is not a function on my camera.

The pictures suggest but do not capture the *pure crazy* spewing from Sally's mouth. This must be what I sounded like the other night in the restaurant.

Sally yells that Derek has betrayed her heart, that she was willing to give up the world for him, that he will never get another woman like her, that she would tear down the walls of the house to be with him; that he is being brainwashed; that he didn't know what he was doing with a woman.

I feel bad for Derek and particularly his sisters, who are witnessing a meltdown that cannot be blamed on love and emotions. Sally probably needs therapy too. Because who throws a plant and tears out grass from the lawn? And who risks getting arrested for not only creating a disturbance and vandalizing property but also statutory rape?

"Sally!" I call out as I approach, dropping my bike and cradling my camera. "Sally, why don't you talk to me?"

She recognizes me immediately.

"Oh, his little boyfriend? You mad that your butt-buddy wants to be with a woman?"

"Sally, I'm sorry about what I pulled at the restaurant the other night."

She curses at me and balls her fists up but doesn't storm off or assault me.

"Sally, you're really upset. But Derek isn't worth going to jail for."

"I'm not going to jail, you tool!"

"Sally, he's *underage.* His sisters are in there watching you trash their front lawn. You should leave now and maybe talk with Derek privately another time."

She curses me out again. I'm impressed by her ability to call me a "fuckputz" without laughing.

I hold my camera a little higher.

"Sally, I have some pictures of you from today. Here on the lawn. Throwing things. It would be bad for you to get arrested and for these pictures to be in the hands of the police." I see her start to breathe and think. She looks at the house, squints. I feel really bad for her. I tell her that I know how it sucks to be mad at someone. I tell her that I see a therapist and that I deal with depression and anxiety.

She seems to be calming down. I feel like being honest and nice has helped. A connection's been made between us that may not mean much, but it might help get her off Derek's lawn.

"Fuck you, you faggot!"

She turns away and yells that her fiancé will tear Derek apart.

"I'll tell him you've been stalking me, Derek! I'll show him the messages you send me! I'll go to the police first!"

I can't see Derek in the window or anything, but I bet he's cringing, worried, maybe laughing, maybe holding his hands over his sisters' ears.

I trot up to Sally and tell her a bold lie.

"There are other pictures. And text messages that Derek has kept."

She looks at me. Some kind of sanity pours over her face.

"You won't prove anything about Derek that he can't disprove," I say calmly. "Just take off. He's not going to call the cops unless you come back to his house. His mom works for the township. It's not going to go well for you."

I'm using a voice I've never been aware I possessed. An adult voice. One that promises and threatens and has the power to do those things.

Sally gets in her Hummer (owned by her fiancé, of course) and leaves.

Derek comes out and thanks me.

"Are we even?" I ask.

"I think so." He looks pale and wounded. "What did you tell her?"

"That you had dirty text messages and pictures."

"How did you know?" He looks embarrassed.

"I just assumed that's what you kids do these days."

Derek tells me not to tell anyone else.

"Are all the pretty ones crazy?" I ask.

"Everyone's crazy," he mutters.

I take this a little personally.

"I take it you two have completely broken up?" I ask.

"Apparently I'm very hard to let go of."

"But you're so undesirable."

"According to who?" he asks.

"The Internet told me."

41.

I HELPED DEREK, for once. This fact rings through my head all weekend. I helped my friend who's always helping me. I helped the guy I always assume needs no one. My fatherless friend whose life has been messy recently because of me. (Well, because of his own crazy choice for romance, too, but also because of me.)

Dr. Bird says I've made a big step in my ability to connect to the outside world.

"Really?" I ask her.

She nods and says I am a passive person discovering active tendencies.

"What do you mean?"

Dr. Bird says sometimes you have to move from a wire with no birds to one with lots of birds.

I tell her that bird metaphors are not her normal method, and she blinks at me.

"I wonder what action you will take next?" she asks, and then attacks the crook of her wing.

I answer that I cannot answer.

Dr. Bird seems dissatisfied with this.

It's Monday morning. My meeting with Miss Tebler dominates my thoughts. To prepare, I read some Whitman and drink a caffeinated iced beverage from Wawa in a seven-second gulp. I skip homeroom and first period to sit and think about what to ask her even though we've never met and I have no idea what she's going to tell me.

When I walk into the administrative suite, Mrs. Berry waves me over with an anxious hand motion.

"She's in her office. I told her you were coming in."

"What do I say? She knows why I'm here, right?"

"Just go in." Mrs. Berry makes herself look busy as a couple of nameless administration-y people walk by. "Go!"

I knock on the door frame of Tebler's office. She looks up at me but does not smile. She's younger than I expected. Almost like she's just graduated from high school, but as I sit down I see degrees from universities.

"What can I help you with today?" she asks. Exactly the question I fear.

Despite my calm morning of bursting confidence, my mind begins to numb. I feel like one wrong question will seal her mouth shut.

"Mrs. Berry thought you might be willing to talk to me about my sister. Jorie."

"But Mrs. Berry also knows," Miss Tebler says, "that I cannot talk about another student with you. Not even about your sister." She folds her hands on her desk and waits for me to ask another question.

"I have been trying to figure some things out," I avoid eye contact. "I talked to the vice principal and he said some things that didn't line up with what Jorie told me and what some other people said."

"Like I said—"

"Can I tell you what *I* know? And maybe you can help me? Just to *help me?* Like, so you wouldn't be betraying confidence or anything?"

"That might be the best way to proceed." She shifts in her old-school-looking leather chair and opens her hands.

I relax slightly.

I say that my home life lacks the warm, sitcom-y feeling that television promised me for years. I say it's cartoonish and grim. Since I don't want her to declare the meeting over due to lack of scholastic relevance, I say that my schoolwork has suffered over the past year because of the chaos in my house.

"Can you tell me what the problem is in the house? Or who?" she asks.

"My dad is a problem. And my mom is a problem. And my sister is a problem because she doesn't act the way my parents think she should act."

Miss Tebler nods but does not take notes. I think about what Dr. Dora might say or do. I think about Dr. Bird. Then Beth, Derek, and Jorie.

"I am also a problem, Miss Tebler. I should be honest. But I want to rectify everything."

I keep things general: how I failed to help Jorie when she needed it, how I made things worse by not taking blame for things I did wrong. I finish by saying that I am doing my best to get Jorie returned to school and welcomed back home in an effort to try to reset the world.

"It might not work," Miss Tebler says. "You say you want things back to the way they were, but things were apparently not very good."

"Things are worse now."

I tell her about Jorie, her friends, her lack of car, furniture, cell phone, joy.

I tell her about my anxieties, my therapy, my need to hug trees.

I feel like my life has become a string of desperate confessions.

"But none of this is really what matters," I finally say. "Because everyone has problems, right? I want to fix something. I want to know *why* Jorie's life got dismantled."

"I'm afraid you have to ask Jorie."

"Miss Tebler, everyone has a different piece of a story and none of the pieces thread together. Or maybe they do and you're the final thread."

Her hands have reclasped.

"James." Miss Tebler looks over at her bookshelf, as if that will help her condescend to me better. "You need to understand. You think that there's a grand explanation for what's happened with Jorie. But there's not a big story. I assure you that even I don't know what Jorie has been through. She didn't tell me any secrets."

We look at each other. Right now I don't know who can be called an enemy and who can be called a friend.

"Do you know why she attacked Gina?"

Miss Tebler says nothing.

"Did you know that I found a box of blades in her closet that she used to cut herself?" My voice rises.

"James, please." It's hard to tell if Tebler knew about Jorie's mutilations.

"How about this: Did you know that my mother broke plastic mixing spoons on my sister's back? Multiple times? That's how hard she hit her. You know that when my sister went upstairs to stare at the welts on her back, I got my sister's butterscotch pudding?"

This upsets me, but it also seems to crack Miss Tebler's armor. There's a protracted silence. I feel my heart pounding in my veins and arteries and muscles and bones.

"James, I wish I could say that I knew how bad things were at home. But I was never *sure.* Jorie came in here to *talk,* but she often never *said* things. If she had told me about abuse or showed me her arms, I would have had no choice but to act. I had hunches, but I could not act on a hunch. It's too dangerous for Jorie and the school and me and you and your parents."

Miss Tebler's pale face convinces me of some kind of honesty, but I'm mad. I'm simply, precisely, acutely, agonizingly *fucking mad.*

"Miss Tebler. This is BULLSHIT!" My eyes burn, my fists clench. I breathe and picture Dr. Bird, who says, "Keep coo, keep coo."

"James, your sister is no longer at this school. It might be that she's better off."

I recall Gina saying the same thing.

My mind pieces things together in a logical fashion. Mrs. Yao pulls Jorie away from an argument in the library and then confronts her in one of the study rooms about her grades. Gina is in the library that day, though she lied to me about being there. Mrs. Yao makes the mistake of asking about Jorie's cut-up arms. Jorie freaks out and throws the laptop or knocks it down or whatever. Enough that it needs to be replaced or repaired. Perhaps this is why VanO knows about the laptop? Mrs. Yao claims she dropped it, though, so there's no reason for anyone to think my sister intentionally destroyed a five-hundred-dollar crap laptop that was out of date four years ago. Then, the next morning Jorie—*for no discernible reason*—attacks Gina. Gina goes to the hospital; Jorie gets expelled. Jorie gets dragged down the staircase and thrown out of our house.

I recall Derek's Rule Number One of Teenage Happiness: *Less detail makes for an easier lie.* Right now all these details signal a very difficult, unhappy lie. But what's the lie? And why was it created?

"Mrs. Berry told me Gina was in the library the day Mrs. Yao found my sister arguing with a couple of kids. Do you know what Jorie was arguing about? Or if Gina was part of it?"

"James, I saw Jorie for about five minutes the day she was

expelled. Nothing she said will confirm your belief that a big plot is at work here."

"Jorie told me she saw Gina the next day and just lost it."

"Why isn't that enough for you?" Miss Tebler asks.

"What's the purpose of beating someone up unless they've pissed you off somehow?"

"You assume that your sister had reason on her side, but what if she was ruled by emotion that day?"

Suddenly, everyone's channeling Dr. Bird and Whitman.

42.

I LOOK ALL OVER the school for Gina. I skip classes hoping that she skips classes and we'll have a great, alone-in-the-middle-of-the-hallway showdown.

No luck.

Toward the end of the day I realize I'm essentially stalking one of the most attractive girls in school. Again. I'm probably not alone in this secret desire to run into her, though I don't go so far as to hang out near bathrooms and the girls' locker room. (Odd how many guys seem to be doing this. Perhaps I should report them?) At least I can claim a more noble goal than simply getting a glance of her nearly perfect form.

It's also strange how many girls at my school seem to look like her from afar—something about hair and height and the confidence people walk with creates a very Gina-like impression. I keep getting tricked. Perhaps my desire to confront her is causing me to confuse her with anyone broadcasting an attractive aura. I start to feel tired and then get distracted by how tired other people look in the hallways. How quickly the laughter-brightness leaves people's faces, allowing lost, sad droopiness to regain control of the muscles.

I've got to *focus.*

As I pass by the senior lounge, which connects to the cafeteria, I hear Gina's laugh. A distinct, semi-infectious sound, it reminds me of all the nights she hung out at our house back when I was little. She and Jorie would cackle endlessly about nonsense. Now when I hear it, I stop short. I have a moment to consider what I want to say, what I should say, and whether I should just keep going.

The old me would choose to hide. The new me pokes my head into the senior lounge.

"Gina," I say, thinking commanding thoughts. "I want to ask you something."

She doesn't get up, roll her eyes, sigh, or make a joke. Nothing. She just looks at me.

"Out in the hallway maybe?" I move my body into the doorway.

"Are you gonna try to beat us all up too?" one of Gina's beautiful minions says.

A witty comeback seems like a good idea, but I am focused on my mental health, my sister, and the truth.

"Go away, James Whitman." Gina remains lounging in the booth with her friends.

"Is this The Cutter's brother?" one girl asks.

"Who?" I'm confused.

"Your sister," Gina quickly explains by pointing at her tiny scar. "We call her The Cutter because of the fight."

Her friends laugh. I realize her friends can help me.

"Oh. Well, I came here to ask you about the library."

"It's down the hall," Gina dismisses. "Keep walking."

"Do you remember that whole thing with my sister and Mrs. Yao?"

"No." Gina sits up. Her eyes seem to glow unnaturally. "What are you talking about?"

"You saw Jorie throw a laptop at Mrs. Yao in the library the day before she pummeled you, right?"

"Did your sister throw a laptop?" Gina asks as if she doesn't know what I think I know she knows I know she knows I know.

I wait.

And I wait and wait and wait and—

"Of course she did!" one of Gina's friends says. "Gina *totally saw* her do it!"

"Shut up, Anne!" Gina barks.

"Wasn't that the day you got into the argument with Darryl and Jenny-Wenny about the shitty weed you sold them?" Anne carries on, somehow enjoying the torment of her beautiful overlord.

"For fuck's sake!" Gina yells.

"Wait, so what did my sister have to do with that?" I ask the helpful Anne.

"Your sister started the whole argument with one of her sarcastic little comments," Anne says. "Caused a whole . . . ruckus. Then Gina overhears your sister tell Mrs. Yao—"

"GET THE FUCK OUT OF HERE!" Gina roars, in a manner unbefitting a future movie star.

The way Gina looks at me and then her friends—the way they look at her—this all seems so small and childish.

My mind fits together explanations. I know why Jorie got expelled for a fight that was no worse than the dozen others that have happened in the school's recent years: she probably tried to squeal on Gina for dealing drugs, but the principal, wanting to protect the school's reputation, didn't believe her. Jorie said *Gina just looked so happy* and it ticked her off. She beats up Gina and the principal expels Jorie and might have even called an unnecessary ambulance to make the fight seem worse!

A conspiracy! An explanation!

Of course, I could also be completely, utterly, totally wrong.

"Thanks, Gina's friends!"

I run out of there as fast as my little feet can carry me, hearing a frustrated growl from Gina Best, who might try to hunt me down for vengeance one day.

43.

A FEW DAYS LATER, as soon as I hear the evil voice on the morning announcements, I know what I have to do. I know what I *can* do.

"Principal Kunkel," I mutter at the speaker while sitting in homeroom. The kid next to me glances quickly my way, but thinks better of making eye contact with the weird guy who appears ready to jump through the speaker.

I cannot look away from his sinister voice. The principal will know it all.

From homeroom I make my way straight to his office. Mrs. Berry sees me, sees my face, and knows not to mess with me.

I exude strength! I've always wanted to *exude!*

He's in his office. I'm in his doorway. He's there with his bloated face and huge eyebrows and folded arms and head full of secrets.

Like Walt says:

It is time to explain myself; let us stand up.

"Principal Kunkel, my name is James Whitman and I'd like to talk to you about my sister."

There's a powerful buzz in my chest. I might be having a heart attack. I might be doing something incredibly stupid. From the look on Kunkel's face, I am.

In his office, the principal doesn't tell me to sit. He chews something in his mouth. Gum or the souls of prior offenders. He walks over to the windows behind his desk and turns his back on me. He looks like he was carved from arrogance and a hairy bar of soap. He's going to talk down to me and I won't be able to respond because the entire office feels like the deepest, coldest ring of hell.

"Mr. Whitman, I know why you're here. But your sister is not coming back to this school. She is not welcome. She will not get her diploma. She had her chance and wasted it. She is not a good person. Or, at least, she is not a person that I want in my school. Violent. Inconsistent academic record. Poor attendance. Consistent lateness."

He waits for me to object, but I keep my mouth shut.

"Good. We agree. Now. I will tell you that your next year in this school will not be easy if you continue to push the issue of her expulsion. You will accept that she is not welcome back and you will not have any problems. You will not bother Mrs. Yao or Mrs. Berry or Miss Tebler or Vice Principal VanOstenbridge."

"Okay."

"Good. Now get out of my office."

I'm pretty sure I know most of what happened, though I am making a crucial assumption about why Jorie attacked Gina.

But I know enough to be here, pushing Kunkel's buttons until he admits something, anything, everything.

"Principal, I have some information that may upset you." My palms sweat and my stomach feels dense. "Gina Best is a drug dealer."

I try to read Kunkel's response. He shows no surprise, which could mean I'm right or very wrong.

"Here's all I want. Jorie walks in graduation. I don't reveal anything about Gina to other teachers, to newspapers, to the Internet." I feel like a character on some crime show.

"Mr. Whitman, you and your sister seem to have the same problem." He turns around and stands behind his desk, arms appropriately folded. "You think you know things and you don't."

He already knows I've been talking to all sorts of people, so he has to believe I know *something.* Then again, maybe I'm so wrong that I'm not a threat.

"Well, what if I went further and said that you know Gina sells drugs and you expelled my sister because she tried to tell you?" Dr. Bird whispers that I should be careful, that I don't have facts, only emotions, that my goals are clear but my methods are dangerous. She puffs up to be noticed. I notice her, but I'm all action right now.

Still, he's too calm. I *am* being disrespectful and he's too calm. The old me would shut down, apologize, cower, look for a way to escape. But the old me is too tired to do a thing to stop the new me.

"How did you and the vice principal find out about Mrs. Yao's laptop? Gina, right? She plays up Jorie's outburst and you have no reason to believe my sister's accusations."

"I have to tell you, James, that you sound crazy. You accuse me of something ludicrous, and it's disrespectful."

"I think there's something ludicrous and shameful about all of this," I continue. "My parents kicked her out of our house and didn't help her at all. They think she's a fuck-up. The only fuck-ups I see are the ones running this school!"

"Watch your tone, Mr. Whitman! If you're trying to earn yourself serious punishment, you are succeeding."

"I'm not earning anything. I haven't hurt anyone or damaged anything! I haven't harmed anyone's reputation. I've tried to clear the record. I'm not sure that's too much to ask, especially since I struggle with depression and anxiety. It's hard enough to get out of bed, never mind talk to people."

"Oh, I love how easy it is for you kids to throw around your emotional problems when you get in trouble. As if it gets you out of things and makes you worthy of explanations! Your sister tried the same thing. Why can't you Whitman kids take a little responsibility for your bad behavior?"

I want to hate everyone involved in this, but that means I have to hate Jorie, too, for hiding truths from me.

"Why all the secrets about Jorie? Why expel her for just a fight when other people fight and come back a week later?"

Principal Kunkel lets out a massive sigh.

"Your sister was arguing in the library with students, then with a teacher. You think no one saw your sister knock over Mrs. Yao's laptop? Your sister was in my office that day because, yes, someone told on her. Not Mrs. Yao, not Gina, but two of the librarian assistants and the librarian. I could have suspended her that afternoon but didn't. I resolved the situation. Miss Tebler and I thought it would be best if Jorie didn't face punishment since she was clearly stressed out and needed help.

"Instead, the next day, your sister sent Gina to the hospital! Come on, Mr. Whitman. Isn't it easy to accept that your sister did something that deserved expulsion? Don't you think I make my decisions carefully?"

I'll probably be imprisoned in some lower realm of the high school forever.

He tells me to leave and that I shall enjoy a month of in-school suspension and some other impressively restrained things.

I had expected him to lose his mind or scream at me, but he must be the kind of guy that bottles up his emotions.

I feel completely defeated.

44.

AFTER SCHOOL, I'M NOT THAT INTERESTED in what Beth and Roy say about the *Amalgam* website. I keep apologizing for not following their enthusiastic ideas. They're kind, though. They explain the timeline for finishing and launching. They tell me that I don't need to do anything except finish a couple more poems.

I nod and nod, tell them impossible things are possible.

"Why don't you just go over and work on your stuff?" Beth says. "You seem like you need to just focus on one thing. Roy and I are all over the place!"

But sitting by myself with a pen and paper seems foolish. I'm a kindergartner staying inside at lunchtime. It's not comfortable. I have no ideas.

I manage half a limerick about Principal Kunkel:

There once was a man named Kunkel

Who learned how to drink like his Uncle,

One week he was wasted

His own piss he then tasted

And . . .

I crumple up the page and the sudden crackle of paper lures Beth to me.

"How you doing over here, chum?" She smiles and sits.

"Just having one of those terrible days."

"Tell me about it."

"You don't want to hear about it." I make a strong effort to avoid eye contact. "Too much lunacy."

"Well, then tell me something good!"

"Nothing's all that good."

"You're here. If things were bad you'd be home or out hugging some trees."

"I guess."

"I'll tell you something good—I dropped *Drama Mavens* like a hot potato!"

It takes a lot to laugh, but I manage it. Strangely, I'm not immediately filled with stupid hopes about hand holding, romantic walks, and smelling her shampoo.

"That's good." I smile. "That's really good."

"You seem less thrilled than I would hope."

"I don't have the capacity to be thrilled right now."

"I needed to not be a part of his life. I need to be in charge of my life. Plus, this way you and I can hang out without guilt and mystery."

I want to jump to conclusions, but I don't.

"I mean, it seems like you need someone to confide in. Whatever that entails. I'm not dumping my boyfriend so we can make out and talk about poetry," she laughs. "But now I can be a better friend, and that's something I want to work on because you're my only real brainy friend, who doesn't look at me weird for running this poetry magazine."

The rabid voice in my head, which usually makes me say too much or hope too much, fails to wrest control of my mouth.

"I guess this all sounds super weird. And you don't seem in the mood to yawp." She smiles, though I only see it from the top edge of my vision since I'm still staring at my pen and paper. "Did I use that right?"

"Yes."

"So, that's good news," she says. "And now your day is a little better! And now you can tell me something good."

"I failed."

"A test?"

"Worse. My sister. I failed Jorie." Here's the moment where I think I could cry and then I realize girls—even girls that like poetry—don't want to see a boy cry.

"I'm sorry, James." Beth has a sweet voice, but I'd rather not be treated like a delicate bird.

"Beth, I feel like everyone is allergic to honesty." I whisper some details about my meeting with the principal, but I don't have the heart to reignite my anger. "I have a month of in-school, which will turn into an entire summer of being grounded. I stole money from my crap job. I can't afford therapy. I can't write any poems. I have no money for film or a new camera. And I forgot to put deodorant on today, so I feel like I stink."

Beth puts her hand on my leg. She doesn't say anything. We could hug. She could kiss my cheek. But this is as much as I can handle right now.

Later I stand around the corner of the pizza shop for twelve and a half minutes. I imagine various scenarios wherein Flip hurts me. The most elaborate ends with me being decapitated with the metal pizza shovel he uses to slip pies in and out of the oven.

Needless to say, he's not pleased that I stole, though he's not even sure how much disappeared from his register. (This works in my favor, since I spent some on therapy.)

I lose my job, of course. That's fair. I am not the kind of kid who believes he can do whatever he wants. At least, I'm trying not to be that kind of kid.

"Don't hold this against Derek, please. He had no idea."

"Of course he didn't. He's not an idiot."

I guess that's the best I can expect. At least I don't love the pizza. No need to find a new place to get slices.

45.

DINNER WITH MY PARENTS. Joy of joys. Sausage in the tomato sauce. Somehow my mother still thinks I won't notice, or that I'll change my mind about the putrid nature of sausage. I don't bother starting an argument since I've been losing arguments lately. I get up to microwave some untainted sauce, but the Banshee informs me that she used the last jar. I put margarine on my noodles and explain to my father, again, that the processed bacon things in the salad are not made from real bacon.

My father asks his usual round of school-related questions: Did I learn anything, what kind of homework do I have, tests coming up, papers to write? He seems more annoyed at the weak curriculum than at me.

"What happened to challenging kids in school? College will kick your ass if you don't prepare."

My father did not go to college, but he is an expert because he reads things on websites and makes up other things that he figures would be true in his perfect world.

This could be a perfect time to bring up my sister. I've already had a freak-out at school, and I lost my job. I can complete my day by driving my parents nuts.

Instead, I eat bland noodles. I shake excess dressing off the iceberg lettuce. I eat cucumbers. I do not talk.

"Dale, I was talking with James a few days ago and thought that maybe we could discuss letting Jorie come back home."

Ah, so much for a quiet, boring dinner.

"Yeah, that's a swell idea." He's already unhappy with dinner—spaghetti being one of his least favorite meals.

"I didn't say we should do it. I just think we should hear what James has to say about it. Maybe it would be good in the long run for our family."

My father puts his fork down. It's still jabbed into a piece of sausage. The image of all the bacteria and animal parts in there makes me squirm. He puts his elbows on the table and puts his palms together and taps his fingers against his lips. He stares at me, even though my mother has triggered the impending doom.

"Your sister cannot live here with our rules. I think we should just let her stay away and be happy with that."

The energy to fight remains dormant. Somewhere, deep inside me, though, I sense a boiling urge to leap at my father and wrap my hands around his throat and tell him that he needs to understand my power. That one day he might wake up and find me, bloody-wristed, at the bottom of the stairs. That one day I might squeeze the life out of his body and mine because I *cannot fucking take it!*

"You have anything to say?" my father, the Brute, asks. "Your mother says this is your idea."

"Whatever you want, Dad. It's your house."

"James, you told me you wanted to talk to your father about this," my mother, the Banshee, argues. "You said he'd listen to me and that you wanted this." Now she's staring at me. "I'm confused."

"I thought it would be nice. But Dad doesn't seem to want Jorie here so, whatever." I start eating faster because I'm going to break down—not in tears. I am dehydrated of sadness. I'm just going to fall asleep for about two weeks and wake up in a hospital with doctors and nurses and parents who have been scared into concern and love for me.

"Listen," my father, the Brute, says, grabbing my recently healed arm, preventing a forkful of salad from entering my mouth. "Your sister is not coming back. I don't even know why you want her back here anyway. She just made this house *unstable.*"

"Remove. Your hand. From my arm." A fleck of pasta flies from my lip to the tablecloth.

He lifts his hand away and apologizes in a mocking tone.

"Mom said she'd talk to you about it because she was okay with it," I lie. Dishonesty can be my weapon too.

"I did not!"

"She said she's still mad and embarrassed about the whole thing." I'm very calm.

"James Whitman, you are *lying!*"

"Mom says you have an evil streak. She says that to lots of people."

See, this is what happens when you have no more energy to yell: you turn your parents against each other.

"Also, Jorie said Mom hits harder than you."

My mother stands, picks up my plate, and throws it at the wall above the kitchen sink, about ten feet away. The resulting sound amazes me. It's the sound of relief, in some sick way. This is exactly the kind of thing my mother is fond of doing, and in a few days she'll deny that she even did it. Just like the bruises on my sister's arms or the terrible things my parents said to Jorie in their blizzards of anger.

With my dinner taken away, I walk upstairs, ignoring the eruptions. I know that my parents are not addressing me, even as the Brute calls me a *spoiled asshole* and the Banshee tells me to *apologize* and the Brute tells her to *tell the truth* and the Banshee says she *can't take living in a house like this with people like this!*

I ignore them.

I'm powerful enough to ignore.

In my room I feel my pulse pound in my eyes. I look at the pictures on my ceiling, my posters, calendar, books, ticket stubs, Little League trophies, clothes on the dresser. All the detritus that surrounds me: they're the first things I see and the last things I see every day. These are the things that maintain my anxieties even though I think they're important and safe and part of me.

The room keeps me sane and crazy. I ask Dr. Bird what to do. Dr. Bird says I need to rearrange the world. The plate-breaking only begins the necessary changes. "Move the pictures. Throw things away. Give things away. Get new clothes. New sheets. Open the windows. Get the dust out."

I find trash bags and rags to wipe away the dust that coats everything. I throw open the windows and breathe in the late-May air. My door is locked and I am a whirlwind, ready to destroy my room.

With trash bags half full and piles of things on my bed in limbo, waiting for me to decide if I can part with them, I stand on my bed and start pulling down my photo tree. The pictures stick together and then one of them rips. I just wanted to take the whole thing down and put it on the wall or something. I just wanted to rearrange it a bit. Now I've ruined the photo tree. I toss it to the floor and feel heat blast my body.

I have to get out of here.

Before I escape, I go into Jorie's room. I take the box of pain out of the closet. I leave it shut, but I hold it in my hands. The weight of it cannot be measured.

I want to burn it. I want to destroy it so that when she comes home Jorie won't be able to prove to herself that she ever cut her skin.

But Dr. Bird tells me that only Jorie can burn the box. This makes perfect sense, so we fly out of the house to take it to her.

46.

"I'M CALLING IN A FAVOR," I say to Derek when he opens his front door.

"Is this a call?"

"I'm calling on you. In the nineteenth-century sense of the word."

"I'd prefer a phone call."

I dial his cell from my cell and we stand, grinning stupidly, before disconnecting and carrying on like semi-adults.

Derek's house always seems dark. Part of that is the wood paneling. But the other part just seems to be the natural aura of his house. Normally I wouldn't be bothered by the dimness, but I ask if we can sit on his back porch, just so I can get the last glimpses of daylight. The walk over has done a lot to calm me.

Derek tells me that Sally hasn't called him at all and he's

had to threaten his sisters with physical abuse so they won't tell on him.

"Seems pretty sad that you are at the whim of your little sisters," I tease, though the idea of him beating his sisters disturbs me, considering everything.

"That's how it works around here. The ladies run the show."

Being outnumbered three-to-one by women must make Derek think about his dad a lot, though he rarely mentions him. Maybe my own father is not so full of shit.

We sit, and there's a discomfort to the silence. *Guys don't sit in silence,* I think over and over. *Guys joke or complain.*

"Are you nervous about graduating?" I ask him.

He answers quickly, refusing to admit to the weakness of anxiety. I hear about how he's excited to be done with high school and how he'll probably go to community college for a while.

"You aren't going to take over the pizza shop, are you?" I ask, making sure my joking disapproval of such a move seems serious.

"Seriously? I could make so much money with a place like that. And I could do it making a better pizza, probably."

"But then you'd be a pizza shop owner. Not the glamorous life we talked about back in the day."

"What did we think we were going to be when we grew up?"

"I think I was going to be a chemist," I say.

"You sucked in chemistry."

"I was just a kid—what did I know?"

"I was going to be a football player," he says. "Then a NASCAR driver."

"You told me once you wanted to be a crossing guard."

"Shut up!" he laughs.

"You did."

"I must have been three or four."

"Yeah, three or four days ago!"

We laugh. I watch the sky get dark. I think about what Derek is thinking about. He's my closest friend and I don't know what he thinks about at dusk, when all the best thinking gets done. Maybe I'm not allowed to know what's in his head. To be fair, he has only been able to piece together little bits of my mangled brain. So, maybe we know each other well enough to stay friends. Maybe knowing too much would *be* too much. And maybe I'll go off to live somewhere and make different friends. Or he'll make new friends or get a new job or move out and have a party-apartment that I can't hang out at because I don't have a car.

I'm making myself sad. Who knows? But things definitely seem to be changing. I can feel it, like the pain of my bones growing faster than my muscles.

"Can you give me a ride to my sister's?" I say after a few minutes of silence.

"After what you did for me, I might give you my car."

"My dad won't even take me to practice driving yet," I laugh. "He took my sister a couple times and then gave up. Said she wouldn't listen. To be fair, I've never asked if he'd take me out. The image of being in the car with my father know-it-alling from the passenger seat—that just doesn't compute."

"I'll take you out to practice."

"Thanks, man," I say. "That'd be a good way to get us both killed."

"Best Friends Die in Horrific Parallel Parking Tragedy."

"Two Traffic Cones in Critical Condition."

Derek drives us to Jorie's as I navigate, working from my bad memory—which means I'm piecing the route backwards and trying to remember landmarks as they speed by in the direction opposite the way I remember them. Does that make sense? It probably shouldn't.

Still, I manage to get us there, and I see Jorie's light on. Who knows if she's home? Part of me wants her to be, and part of me wants her to be out at a new job, smiling, making new friends, impressing people with her sociability and pep.

Derek lets me sit in the car for a minute, quietly (though the radio is thumping out some crazy song he seems to know).

"Can I ask you something?" he says finally.

"Yeah?"

"You're not going in there to stab yourself to death or anything?"

"No!"

"And you're not going to stab her to death?"

"Shut up." Dr. Dora would chastise us both for laughing about mental illness. But I have to admit, it feels nice for someone else to make light of things.

"So what are you contemplating, then?" he asks.

"I'm just figuring out what I should lie about."

"Honesty's the best policy."

"Sounds like a kindergarten teacher's bumper sticker."

"Apparently my dad used to say it all the time."

I say it's a good philosophy. Dr. Bird agrees (though Derek doesn't hear that part). I get out of the car with Jorie's box of pain held in my hands. I tromp up the steps, loud enough to signal my approach.

When Jorie opens the door, my brain begins assigning adjectives. *Tired* seems inadequate. *Haggard?* Too chimney-sweep.

Fatigued? She probably has not run any races lately. *Tuckered out?* She's not a five-year-old. *Weary?* Maybe. *Zonked?*

Yes.

"You look zonked," I say.

"Zonked?" she asks, zonkedly.

"You know. Tired."

"Why didn't you just say *tired* then?"

"Would Walt Whitman use such a plain word?"

We're having this whole exchange with me on the porch and her inside as a few bugs flitter over my head before dive-bombing my eye or nose. Perhaps it's this that tells her to let me in, as she finally steps back and makes an elaborate arm-wave to point the obvious way.

Her apartment has furniture now. A couch, two cheap construct-them-yourself chairs, a huge saucer-shaped wicker seat, and a small table in front of the couch that seems too high, but as there's still no TV, it probably doesn't matter.

"Fancy!" I comment. I am much too hyper to have a serious conversation. I'm still not even sure what conversation to have with her.

Jorie paces. It's not an orderly path. It's just movement. She picks up a book and puts it somewhere else. She folds a few pieces of clothing that are on her bed, then smells them and tosses them in a laundry basket.

She finally sits herself down in the wicker saucer. The high-pitched squeaks of the wicker seem out of place.

"Sorry, I'm just having a bit of a panic attack," she admits.

I brace myself for talk of money woes, potential homelessness, suicidal thoughts, and a newspaper headline about a local girl living under suburban bridges just a few miles from her parents' house.

"This guy was supposed to call me today and he didn't. Stupid stuff." She relaxes a bit in the weird wicker chair.

"I thought you were going to say something completely different." I tell her about the headline.

"Jeez, I thought I was a pessimist!" She grins. "I'm sorry. I freaked out when I heard the car because I thought this guy was going to come over. But it was just you."

I make a mock-offended face.

"Not that a visit isn't nice!"

"How was this guy gonna call?"

"Oh! I got a new phone." She struggles to extricate herself from the saucer chair but gives up quickly. "Can you grab it? It's on the kitchen counter."

I do, and the phone looks like one of the kind that people get when they can't afford the one in the commercials. Still, it's better than nothing.

"I'm glad you've got a phone again. It'll be nice to get in touch with you easier."

"Totally. Without my phone and e-mail and junk, I just totally don't talk to anyone unless I see them. It felt good for a little bit—to talk to people face-to-face. People have to make more of an effort that way."

She may be talking about us, too, but I'm just so happy that I'll have a direct connection to her again. Assuming she can keep paying the phone bill.

She tells me about her new job. It sounds like her old job, just a different cuisine and better tips.

"It's a upper-tier chain, I guess. There's some nonsense industry ranking system that the manager talks about. I'm not even sure. But the people there are nice and there's less drinking on the job, so less shenanigans."

Jorie interrupts my thought when she finally notices her box of pain, semi-tucked in my sweatshirt.

"Whoa. Why do you have that?"

I open my sweatshirt more and look down at my guilty hands.

"I brought it over so you could destroy it."

"That was hidden in my room."

"I know."

Even though I did something wrong by going through Jorie's stuff, I don't want to apologize for digging out the small tumor in the closet.

"Why did you go in my room?"

"I didn't go looking for it." I sit on her uncomfortable, cat-odor-y couch. (It should be noted that Jorie does not have any cats.) I feel itchy.

"It didn't fall out of my closet on purpose, James. Give it to me!" She takes it and doesn't look at it or hold it close to her body. She places it in the kitchen on the counter, then, perhaps thinking that the light in there is too bright, she places it on the floor on the other side of her mattress.

"I was looking for poems for the literary magazine and I thought it had poetry inside."

Jorie starts pinching her arm. She's not screaming or crying or banging around her apartment.

I ask if she's okay; she says not to change the subject.

"Jorie, *I know.* I opened something I shouldn't have. I brought it here because I want you to destroy it, though. I want you to promise me you'll do something to stop hurting yourself. That's all I want to say about it."

"You don't understand. I can't explain it."

"I know. I just thought the gesture—setting it on fire, or

something—would be nice. But I was in a bad mind-set when I left home to come here tonight. Probably not a good idea to burn things in this mind-set."

"That box. James, there's some things that other people shouldn't know," she says.

I wait for more but nothing follows.

"I worry about you," I say.

"I don't want you to worry about me. I don't want to think that every time I do anything it might make you worry."

"I can't help it," I say. "But doesn't it feel better to know someone cares about you?"

"No!" She's serious. "I can barely care about myself. But I don't want you to take that personally. I haven't been Super-Communicating Girl. It's not because I don't want to be there for you. I just only have so much of myself that I can give."

I am okay with this because it's better than guessing about her feelings.

We talk about music and laugh a little. I tell her about Derek's love life; she doesn't believe how I saved the day with the threat of blackmail.

All the while my brain urges me to bring up Gina Best and that whole mess, but I don't want to ruin the night or trigger another panic attack that destroys us both.

Still, what feels like curiosity on my part might actually be necessity.

"We don't have to talk about this, but I tried to blackmail the principal. I told him I knew he knew Gina was a drug dealer. I thought he'd freak out and let you walk at graduation, at least." I look at her ceiling. "It didn't work. Plus Mom and Dad won't let you move back home."

"James!" She's got my attention but still yells my name. Then, her voice is normal. "I don't want to go back home. Please tell me I'm being heard."

"I hear you." We are making eye contact. Fixed, strong, important. We are hearing each other, seeing each other.

"I just feel like it was always me against you guys," she says. "I know it's not on purpose. They just always made you out to be on their side."

"I'm sorry." This apology feels necessary.

"It's not really your fault. Why would you back me up when it would just piss them off more? I get it. In the grand scheme of things, it makes sense. You protect yourself by agreeing with them or just not arguing with them. But I hope you understand that it *really* messed me up. I have all these things I never thought I could tell anyone."

"I think you could have told me some things. Maybe not

everything. But I've been going nuts trying to just figure out what happened when you got kicked out. It's like no one thinks I can handle it."

"Why?"

"Please tell me there's a big conspiracy or something." I'm serious and also kidding. "I need to know that all my obsessing was worth it."

"You might be disappointed."

I go right to the key question: "Why the hell did you beat up Gina Best?"

Jorie looks up at the ceiling. I know the impulse—answers live on ceilings. When she looks at me again I can see that the answer requires controlled emotions.

"She overheard me talking to Mrs. Yao. She told a couple of her friends that I was a psycho who cuts herself. It was . . . I couldn't even tell *you.*"

I feel sick. The Cutter! Gina and her damn friends joked about it and I believed Gina when she said it was just because Jorie beat her up.

"I'm *so, so, so* sorry," I whisper.

"I should've told you." She blows her nose and throws away the tissues, then returns to her seat with the box of pain. "It wasn't Gina's place to tell anyone, but that's the way she is. She says what she wants. So one of her friends says something to me and I track her down and she's oblivious. So I tried to beat the crap out of her."

Jorie says Kunkel threatened her for sending Gina to the hospital.

"Why didn't you just tell him Gina was selling drugs in the library the day before?" I ask, recalling what Gina's friends so easily revealed in the senior lounge the other day.

"Who told—? Never mind," Jorie says. "If I ratted Gina out, why would he believe me?"

"So is that why he expelled you?"

"I told him to expel me, James." Jorie bends her left fingers against the palm of her right hand. I hear quick pops and cracks.

"You *asked to be expelled?*" I can't believe it.

"I wasn't going to make it. I wasn't sleeping, I wasn't doing my work. I was full of angry thoughts anytime someone looked at me. I felt hyper-visible even though most people didn't know who I was until I was expelled."

"Didn't you think that Mom and Dad would freak when you got expelled?"

"They kicked me out for a thousand reasons. It doesn't matter why." She ponders the box of pain on her lap. She doesn't look me in the eyes, then she does, then she doesn't.

"I didn't really have some grand plan, James. It's just a bunch of stuff that happened. When Mrs. Yao asked me about my arms . . . I just felt like my life was so stupid and miserable." She rolls her hand as if I've heard all of this already, though I haven't. "Getting expelled and kicked out let me work full-time. I earned money and got this apartment. I stayed with some friends and cried for about two weeks straight, first, but I manage. Kind of."

"So is that why Gina went to the hospital for no reason? To make it seem like you beat her up really bad and make the expulsion seem more valid or something?"

"No idea." Jorie shrugs.

"Why didn't the principal just *tell* me this? I thought there was some huge conspiracy!" I rub my eyes. "I feel like such an idiot!"

"Maybe he didn't want anyone to know that I volunteered to leave? So he keeps his authority?"

Whatever the case, Jorie achieved an escape in the heat of anger and shame. She could have been immobilized, but instead she acted to defend and even define herself.

I'm being forced to do the same. I'm not going to survive another year at home if I spend it in my room. I need to be out in the world. I need to appreciate the people around me. I need to actually care about myself, as lame as that sounds.

I can't keep pretending like my life isn't worth living. It hasn't even fucking started yet.

I must look zonked, because Jorie gets me a glass of water and a beer.

"Take your pick," she says.

I turn down the beer, afraid that my return home will already be a mess without Pabst Blue Ribbon on my breath.

"Are you seeing my therapist yet?" she asks. "She really helps me when I can get over there."

I tell her a bit about Dr. Dora, though not too much. That feels like something I want to keep on the edge of mystery. To keep it powerful. If I go around talking about therapy, I'll end up destroying the effect it has.

"How does Dr. Bird feel about it?" Jorie smiles.

"Dr. Bird is always around."

"I'm glad Mom and Dad are paying for you to go. They always told me it was a waste of money and blah blah blah."

"They don't know," I admit. "I got a job to pay for it. I had a job, anyway. I'll get a new one and keep going."

"That's good! I never thought I had the ability to do that—to take care of myself. I always felt like I needed permission to do good things for myself, even just to buy new shoes or something. I never knew how to do stuff."

Jorie looks at me. I expect a smile, but there's just a soft look on her face. I feel like she's a little proud of us. That we've survived so far.

"James, I needed to get out of there. This looks like a shitty place to live and junk, but for me it's *better.* I am a paycheck away from being homeless most of the time, but for me that's better. Because then I know whose fault it is if things go sour. I don't know if moving out of the house will be good for you. But I couldn't spend another day trying to figure out all the invisible rules that Mom and Dad made up and changed. I tried telling them about things and they just talked right over me." She makes a gesture around her head. "It's like they don't believe my brain works different from theirs."

"I just thought that if you came back home that it might be easier for both of us. Us versus them, you know?"

"I know. But it wouldn't really be that. They treat you different."

"They pretend I'm okay."

"You will be okay."

"I think we'll both be okay."

We probably should hug and cry or something, but we sit there in silence for a bit, sipping drinks, being alone together. Comfortable. Almost like adults, but sort of like when we shared a room as kids and we couldn't fall asleep. We both knew we were awake but we didn't always say anything. It was not a profound silence. Just nice.

I text Derek:

I NEED YOU TO HELP CLEAN
UP ALL THE PEOPLE I JUST
MURDERED.

I think I can hear him laughing his ass off.

47.

DEREK DROPS ME OFF at an hour that many parents would consider decent, though maybe not on a school night. Still, it's not yet midnight, and my parents begin talking at me like I've come home from a rave with the stink of sweat and confusion and thumping beats.

They talk at me from the kitchen table, where much teeth-gnashing has apparently happened since my departure. Instead of fleeing upstairs, I go to the fridge and get the components for a peanut butter and jelly sandwich. I glance at the kitchen sink and see that the plate discus has not been cleaned up.

"I don't think you understand what we're trying to say, here, kiddo," my mom says in that strange way she merges casual words with a stern angry voice.

My father cuts in. His words do not register as language in

my mind. Instead, I think about how no one in Whitman's poetry ever seems angry. He never sounds like he's going to catch on fire. Surely Whitman had arguments; surely he saw people yelling, frustrated, angry. But he didn't bother putting it in poetry. It's as if the energy couldn't be captured. Or, better, it wasn't worth capturing.

So, I spread jelly and peanut butter and cut my sandwich diagonally because I've seen it done that way but never done it myself. I stand and eat my sandwich. My parents seem confused by my lack of response. Especially because I'm not just staring at my food like a quiet participant, nodding along as they badmouth my sister or yell at me for some minor infraction. I'm eating, making eye contact, not speaking, not agreeing.

I must be quite unnerving.

"And if you think your sister is coming home, you are dead wrong," my father growls. "She's proven incapable of living here."

I eat a potato chip and then clear my throat.

"Well?" my father says.

"That's not a problem," I say. "She doesn't want to come back here."

"Why not?" my mother asks.

"She's *not allowed* back here," my father asserts.

"No. She made the decision. She's gone for good." I continue eating. "And you should know that she got expelled on purpose. That's how much she hated living here."

I don't go so far as to say Jorie hated *them.* I'm not sure if that's to save myself some trouble or to spare a little part of my parents' feelings. Or maybe to avoid putting words into Jorie's mouth. She could hate them. She could also be indifferent to them. That might actually hurt my mother the most, but it's not my place toss out insults on Jorie's behalf.

My mother's face suggests she's not happy that people might know her house is bad enough that one of her kids would prefer to be branded an expelled loser.

My father tries, again, to assert that he has the power to ban her or welcome her.

I make one last attempt to explain.

"I need to say something to both of you. Jorie is gone, and it was her decision. I am not in the best shape mentally, either. What you need to do is to promise you will help me get better. I am seeing a therapist and I cannot afford to pay for it all by myself. I will pay some, but I want you to help out."

My father begins objecting.

"HEY!" I yell. The volume of my voice goes to eleven.

I have everyone's attention. Even the foundation of the house waits for me to speak.

"This is not really negotiable. I have serious issues that I need to talk to a professional therapist about. I have already gone a few times, but I can't make enough money to go see her on a regular basis."

"You can tell us what's wrong," my mother says with conviction.

"No. I really can't."

I tell them that we just don't have that kind of family. Some families might share things and support each other through emotionally rough times. That's not us. But I stop before it seems like I hate them. I have reasons I can cite in support of hatred, but I'm not ready to do that. It seems counterproductive since I'm going to get them to pay for my therapy.

"You kids," my father begins. "You kids think it's so hard. You think you have all these things to be depressed about."

"That's not it, Dad. It's not a rational thing. It's not that I don't *know* I have an okay life. A place to live, clothes, friends. It's my brain and my body. I'm wired funny. I can't help it. I need to learn how to think and feel. So stop telling me that I'm being depressed on purpose. I can't *fucking help it.*"

My father's face doesn't change, so I assume he doesn't understand. Without another objection or insult, he lopes upstairs. I expect him to hurl down a punishment like a lightning bolt from Zeus. Instead, nothing.

My mother stays at the table until I'm done eating. She moves to take my plate and I tell her I'll clean it up.

"The one in the sink, too," I say.

"You don't know what it's like," she says. I do not see sadness or tears. I see that she's insulted, and trying to believe she knows better than I do. I'm being condescended to.

I repeat that I'll clean up the mess.

She lingers, then leaves.

At the sink I stare at the spaghetti sauce stains and plate pieces. The easy thing to do is turn on the faucet and wipe all the small pieces into the mouth of the drain. Enough would escape to make it work, but there'd always be little pieces in the gunk of the plumbing. Little pieces would snag on other things being washed away. So it makes more sense, despite the plodding, painful pace, to pick each stray piece up one by one for the next hour.

It will help me practice patience.

It will give me time to calm myself.

I begin and think of all the ways I could make a poem out of this—one that's lively, hopeful. One that describes the risks of cutting my arms with each plate piece before they're melted like ice by the tap water. One that's about me but also about everyone that suffers, even if the suffering seems too big or fake.

It doesn't seem possible; but maybe it's just not easy.

48.

AMERICA! I SING to the tiny part of you that I call home. The square feet that I sleep upon, tromp upon, shower upon, sweat upon.

I sing in the morning, yawp! Yawp!

I ache in the evenings when I think of things that I may miss.

I yearn to walk barefoot in the grass like I did in the days when things meant little.

I miss the days when things meant little and things were all so big compared to me.

But, still, America, I have the little parts of you to love.

I stop and stare and contemplate leaves of grass. I hug your trees, I look on maps for creeks. I smile at men who fish off unnamed bridges into brown rivers.

I delight in the meals my mother cooks, begrudged, but at least I do not find your dead animals in my food, nesting in noodles and broccoli spears.

I delight in my father's moodiness, his concern, as I go off to learn to drive with Derek.

I delight in independence!

America! You are too much for me to know. I will only see little bits of you. I will never know your thoughts. I will never know the depths of your depressions or the truth behind your mania. Just as you will never know me. I will always be too small. I will always need assistance.

But I celebrate the people who have sprung forth from you.

I celebrate the seniors who whoop, carefree, close to the new beginning. I envy them, thinking of how Jorie spoke so well of the freedom that seems like poverty to me.

I celebrate the geeks that don't know how to dress right or walk right. The ones that say they don't read poetry or listen to music. The ones carrying their weight in textbooks, studying for tests that will repeat for years. Studying the little music that makes our bodies work or the world work. I admire their complexity, their mysterious language, their awkward haircuts and inside jokes.

I celebrate the girls, who stroll through the halls in skirts and shirts and secret grins that distract me, fill me with lust and hope and secret grins of my own. There is nothing wrong with me. I am only reacting to bright sunshine; I am covered in skin that has become self-aware.

I celebrate the athletes who have some way to express themselves, even though the things they say may sound like argles, blurbs, murmurs, grunts. They yawp. They yawp!

I celebrate the people lost, looking for friends, losing them, making them. I look people in the eye and see all the faces turning away. I celebrate our shared shyness, the worry of seeing something honest in the face of someone else.

I celebrate Mrs. Berry for trying. Miss Tebler for trying.

I celebrate Dr. Bird, for cooing me through tough times, for being the part of me that hopes.

I celebrate Dr. Dora, who tells me to breathe and write and not to worry about worry. Who tells me I don't have to pretend to be hopeful, who tells me I can be depressed, who tells me I can survive, not that I must survive.

I celebrate the hope of medicine and the hope that I will not need it, even when I feel like I need it. I celebrate the process of deciding; I celebrate the ability to take my time to know, despite yearning for calm during long nights of unprovoked anxieties.

I celebrate Derek, who will make new friends but—and I am sure of this—will not leave me behind or brush me aside. I am like his brother, but not. Important, but different.

I celebrate Beth, who will be my friend and reads my poems and tells me to cheer up when I'm teetering on the edge, but who does not tell me to get over it when I have fallen down. I celebrate all the possibilities of our friendship and how we have all the time and space to figure out how much more it can be.

I celebrate Jorie, who lives, suffers, sends me photographs of trees, tells me when she's sad instead of assuming I do not need to know her weakness. I celebrate the ashes of her pain box, kept in a new box in her apartment, with the words on the outside: *I answer that I cannot answer.*

And I celebrate all the people who read the *Amalgam* and talked about it and shared it on the Internet. I celebrate them because they celebrated Beth and Roy and all the work they did. And even me—they sang of me! Were surprised by me, felt they'd discovered me. Uncovered me. Remembered me. It will all fade in September. I will go back to being just a face in the hallway. But I sang for a little while and some of them heard me and felt enough to say they felt something similar.

I cannot ask for more, America! I cannot ask for anything!

I only wish to wake each morning with enough strength to sing!

In my own voice, I sing!

Of my self, I sing!

Yawp!

Acknowledgments

A billion thank-yous to the following excellent humans: my agent, Sara Crowe, for her warmth and belief. Margaret Raymo, for clarity, great ideas, and caring about the pieces as much as the whole. To everyone at Houghton Mifflin Harcourt for seeing potential in James, Jorie, and Dr. Bird and sending out their barbaric yawp with me.

Thanks to the Rutgers Newark MFA faculty for dedication, skill, honesty, and care. Jayne Anne Phillips, Tayari Jones, and Alice Elliot Dark each taught me very important things about writing and the writing life. Also, thanks to my wonderful fellow graduates Erin MacMillan, Scott Bowman, Chidi Asoluka, Paul Vidich, Amy Kiger-Williams, Saeed Jones, Aimee Rinehart, Mauro Altamura, Owen Duffy, Brett Duquette, Melissa Aranzamendez, Ryan McIlvain, and many, many, many others.

Thanks to the following journals for publishing my short fiction over the years: *Reed, Granta, Narrative, Stymie, Hummingbird Review, StoryQuarterly,* and *BestFiction.org.*

Thanks to Kerri Arsenault for guidance and perspective during the long, spiraling query adventures.

Thanks to the English Department of Rowan University, particularly Cindy Vitto, Cathy Parrish, and Barbara Patrick. Thanks also to the Rutgers Camden University English Department, especially Dee Jonzak, Tyler Hoffman, Chris Fitter, Joe Barbarese, Lisa Zeidner, Geoff Sill, Bob Ryan, and Rafey Habib.

To my handful of patient, quirky, book-nerd, cartoon-loving friends: Phaedra, Tom and KC, Mike and Vicki, Buddy, Rob, Steve, Morgan and Declan, Tom, Daitza, Erik Smith, Sarah Brookover, and Andrew Panebianco.

Going way back, thanks for friendship, no matter the ups or downs: John Garretson and Sappa James. I root for your happiness.

To Colin, Ed, Marcy, Mike, Chris, and the rest of the Grooveground crew (past and present) for allowing me to commandeer the same table and chair for three years (and counting).

Thanks to Kathryn Kopple, Tracy Strauss, Louise Tolmie-

Pollack, Mike Scalise, and the entire Breadloaf Experience (which is not a Jimi Hendrix cover band that exclusively plays the Breadloaf Writers Conference).

Thanks to Rick Moody, for inspiration as well as for listening and responding when there's so much music that would be more fun to listen to and talk about.

Thanks, Alicia Bessette, for knowing the importance of sunlight.

Thank you, Matthew Quick, for advice and guidance, honesty, disagreement, forgiveness, ideas, support, and a thousand other things that cannot be easily summed up.

Thanks to Dana Harrison, for strength, brilliance, sarcasm, exasperation, and being a true, unapologetic book nerd.

A trillion thank-yous to my parents; to Rin and Fred; to Lynne and Bill; to Dave, Mike, Mat, and Laurie, and to the rest of my family.

An extra and infinite thank-you in the form of a photograph or a song or a hug to my sister, Rin. She's the best person to drive around New Jersey with because she knows when to slow the car down so I can take photos of rust and decay and trees. That and a bunch of other reasons that do not need to be typed here.

Thank you, Sable, who can't read this because she's a dog.

Thank you, Dean-the-bean, who can't read yet but will learn soon.

Finally, to my wife, Laura, who believes and supports and reads and edits and questions and, most important, still laughs. Thank you thank you thank you! Let's keep laughing.